the
crayon
messages

the
crayon
messages

christine thackeray

✸ a visiting teaching adventure

CFI

Springville, Utah

The views expressed within this work are the sole responsibility of the author and do not necessarily reflect the position of Cedar Fort, Inc., or any other entity.

This is a work of fiction. The characters, names, incidents, places, and dialogue are products of the author's imagination, and are not to be construed as real.

ISBN 13: 978-1-59955-148-7

Published by CFI, an imprint of Cedar Fort, Inc., 2373 W. 700 S., Springville, UT 84663
Distributed by Cedar Fort, Inc., www.cedarfort.com

LIBRARY OF CONGRESS CATALOGING-IN-PUBLICATION DATA

Thackeray, Christine.
 The crayon messages / Christine Thackeray.
  p. cm.
 ISBN 978-1-59955-148-7 (alk. paper)
 1. Young women—Fiction. 2. Older people—Fiction. 3. Mormons—Fiction.
I. Title.
 PS3620.H33S57 2008
 813'.6—dc22

                                    2007052897

Cover design by Nicole Williams
Cover design © 2008 by Lyle Mortimer
Edited and typeset by Annaliese B. Cox

Printed in the United States of America

10 9 8 7 6 5 4 3 2 1

Printed on acid-free paper

WE MUST CHERISH ONE ANOTHER, WATCH OVER
ONE ANOTHER, COMFORT ONE ANOTHER AND GAIN
INSTRUCTION, THAT WE MAY ALL SIT DOWN IN
HEAVEN TOGETHER.

—Lucy Mack Smith

contents

acknowledgments

This project had such a unique beginning that it would have died completely if it had not been for the continued support of my brilliant sisters. To Jaroldeen Romero, who saw in the original the true heart of my message. To Patricia Oveson, who also read every word and gave me her two cents, which has been worth much more. To Catherine Tryon, the namesake of my main character, who is so filled with love that people are drawn to her. To Marianna Richardson, whose keen intellect and accomplished example lifted me to try again after multiple rejections. And to my mother, Jaroldeen Edwards, who showed me that despite having a large family and heavy church and civic responsibilities, we can still reach for our dreams.

I've also got to mention my children, who threw in multiple dialog and plot suggestions to spur their mother on—some of which were used and others simply laughed at. Lastly, I must thank my dear husband, Greg, who put up with dirty dishes and laundry mountains while his wife wrote late into the night. He is a true companion in every sense of the word, and his loving encouragement is my life's breath.

❋ the letter route

Looking down at the list again, Cath sighed. Rather than actually visit these sisters, she had been told specifically just to send notes, but something in her couldn't do it. A letter seemed so impersonal. No, she had to at least talk to them once, and then, if they wanted, she would send the monthly letters as asked.

Her finger traced the first line of the paper and rested on the name of her companion. The Relief Society secretary said the computer wouldn't let her leave the space empty so she stuck in Gwen Keen's name—but Hillary Jacobs had made it very clear to Cath that she should just ignore Gwen's name altogether and write the letters. Cath didn't like the idea of ignoring anyone, and perhaps it was the secretary's matter-of-fact dismissal of an actual person that wouldn't allow her to simply fulfill the "letter" of the law. Cath envisioned a lonely little woman, sitting by herself in a sterile room, and wanted to cry. It haunted her all the way home from church, and so as soon as the family was fed and dinner cleared, she ran for the phone while most of them were napping.

Picking up the receiver and dialing, she felt a twinge of nervousness, but before she had time to back out, a gruff voice answered, "Pleasant Valley Home for the Elderly."

"May I please talk to Gwen Keen? She's a resident there."

"Not likely, but hold on," the harsh voice commanded, followed by a long silence.

After about five minutes, a gentle voice drifted through the ear piece. "I'm Gwen. Who is this?" It is interesting how age affects people's voices. Some women almost sound like men as they get older; others get raspy or cranky like a wicked witch. But Gwen's voice reminded Cath of an innocent child, and she couldn't wait to meet her.

"My name is Cath Reed. I'm new to the ward and was just called to be your visiting teaching companion," she said as brightly as possible. "Is there a time I can come visit with you?"

"Oh, I would love that. When are you coming? I haven't really talked with anyone for months now. It would be wonderful to meet you. Cath, is it?"

Cath assured her she would drop by that night and again on Tuesday. Gwen laughed with joy. "I can hardly wait. I'll try to stay awake until you get here."

How sweet, Cath thought. As she hung up, she planned on using Gwen's loneliness and enthusiasm as leverage to accomplish her task. She looked down at the other six names, but there was only one that she recognized—Jerri Miller, the bishop's wife. She had never actually met her, but she'd overheard in a conversation that Jerri had stopped coming a few years ago because she was offended by someone at church. Cath loved her new bishop, his patient smile and quiet manner, and she could relate to the feeling of being offended. It had been two months since she'd moved in, and not a single sister had reached out or made any effort to befriend her. Well, that wasn't exactly true.

The first week, Tandy Kates had dropped by and invited her to go jogging. Cath had wanted to get in better shape but hadn't exercised regularly—ever. But after the miserable three-mile marathon and Cath's heel full of blisters, Tandy had never called back, and, worse still, she seemed to avoid Cath at church. If anyone else had even made an effort to say hello, it may not have hurt so much. Cath secretly wondered if she would ever be able to call this place home. Swallowing bravely, she dialed, and the phone was answered on the first ring with a curt, "Hello, Jerri Miller here."

"Hi," Cath said. "You don't know me, but I'm Cath Reed. I moved into the ward a few months ago and have been assigned to be your visiting teacher—"

"Don't worry about it," Jerri interrupted her blandly. "Just send me another letter like they always do."

"No!" The violence of her own reaction surprised her. "I want to meet you." Cath tried to soften her tone. "Since I have moved into this ward your husband has been such a gift to me and my family that I would love to talk with you in person."

"I don't want to become someone's project—," she began.

"Actually, I'm sort of asking you to do a project on someone else. I just got off the phone with Gwen Keen at the nursing home, who is my companion. I was hoping we could meet in her room so that she could feel more involved since she can't make it to church. When I spoke to her, she sounded so lonely that I told her I would make it over there tonight. I know it's short notice, but she was so excited to have visitors. Would you mind?" Cath bit her lip, wondering if she was pushing it too hard, and the pause that followed did nothing to help relieve her anxiety. Then after a few moments Jerri responded, "You say you talked to Gwen? Aren't you a clever one? I'll be there at seven. See you then," and hung up.

Cath's success encouraged her to call another. She dialed the next name, Alexia Brown, and got the answering machine. After leaving a message, she continued down the list. Two sisters could meet her that night and one more on Tuesday. One woman hung up as soon as she said she was from the Church, and Cath wrote "letter" next to her name. But only one out of six (with one no-show) was great odds. Feeling victorious, she hurried to throw together an evening snack for the family and freshen up before leaving for the nursing home.

A few hours later, Cath walked into the front foyer of the Pleasant Valley Home for the Elderly, where a few residents in wheelchairs chatted happily with each other. The rooms seemed to be behind a large glass partition, where a burly nurse sat at a desk, talking on the phone. She had thick light brown hair pulled back in a no-nonsense ponytail at the base of her neck. Her round face gave no hint of her age, for she had neither wrinkles nor the bright enthusiasm of youth. The short, stocky woman scowled and reminded Cath of her middle school P.E. teacher who emotionally tortured her for an entire year because she couldn't make it to the top of the climbing rope. Miss Mabel forced her to try every day in front of the whole class. Cath never did get more than halfway up, and it was still a sore spot even after all these years. Looking at her name tag, Cath was relieved. The nurse's name was Sonja, but she still couldn't shake the feeling of being just a bit intimidated. Turning around, she saw the clock on the wall and realized there were fewer than ten minutes before Jerri Miller would arrive, so Cath forced herself to walk up to the desk and face the nurse.

Trying to look as mature and sophisticated as she could, Cath announced, "I'm here to visit with Gwen Keen. I just talked to her a couple of hours ago and she is expecting me."

"You talked to Gwen? I don't think so," said the nurse rudely.

"No, I did, Sonja." Cath hoped using her first name would make a difference. "She really is expecting me."

"Gwen is sleeping." The nurse shooed her away and went back to work. At first Cath wanted to leave, but the thought of Gwen's lonely voice turned her back around. Cath knew she was on the Lord's errand and said a little louder, "I have another friend who is planning on meeting me here to see her in about fifteen minutes. Could we let her sleep until she comes and then try to wake her?"

The nurse slammed down her pen and stood up impatiently.

She was a good three inches shorter than Cath, and suddenly Cath felt much more confident. The nurse stared at her and rolled her eyes. "You mean, you don't know?" she said flatly.

Cath shook her head. "What?"

"Miss Keen has a rare form of narcolepsy called Kleine-Levin syndrome. She sleeps for days, sometimes weeks, without waking up. Then she'll have maybe an hour or two when she is lucid before she drops back off again. She would be dead if we didn't feed her intravenously. So there is no use visiting her; she is asleep." The nurse plopped back down triumphantly and picked up her pen, thinking the subject was closed.

"Oh." Cath lowered her head, visibly disappointed, but she just couldn't let it go. Her only hope was to explain it all, and so she began, "Actually, I am from Gwen's church and recently moved to the area. We have a program where we visit with our members in their homes. Gwen was assigned with me to visit a number of women who have all agreed to meet here tonight and Tuesday to visit with her. These are ladies that rarely come, and if Gwen were awake, I know she would want them to have this experience . . ." she trailed off, ready to leave in defeat.

The nurse looked at Cath with raised eyebrows and then laughed out loud with a raspy smokers' laugh. "Let me get this straight," she snickered. "You are new, and the ladies from the Mormon Church, who probably knew exactly what they were doing, strapped you with a totally incoherent visiting teaching companion and a bunch of inactives? That is rich. What did you do to get on their bad side?" She chortled again.

Cath had never looked at it that way and wondered if there could be any validity to the nurse's words. "How did you know I'm—"

"A Mormon?" The nurse lowered her eyes, her tone turning bitter. "Just look at you. You know, I went to Primary and Mutual. Heck, I'm even a seminary graduate, but I'm never going back. It's a long story." The naked hate in her face made Cath's heart ache.

"I am so sorry." Cath met her eyes gently, seeing in them the hurt that had shaped the nurse for so many years.

The nurse suddenly softened and pushed a button on her desk, buzzing her in. "The best revenge is success. Get 100 percent," she encouraged. "It's the third door to the left."

The residents' rooms looked exactly like the rooms in every other nursing home Cath had ever been in, with the combined smells of old urine, medicine, and cheap gravy trapped in the commercial-grade linoleum. When she came to the Gwen's room, it was barren of any personal items. Cath's shoes echoed with each step as she walked up to the lone bed. Gwen lay there peacefully like an ancient Sleeping Beauty. Her hair was snow white, but her warm skin was surprisingly smooth. Her features were delicate, and Cath felt a tingling all over her body as she stood there, as though this was exactly where she was supposed to be. She wanted desperately to speak with this woman face to face, just once, and felt somehow she was in the presence of greatness. But from what the nurse said, it could be weeks, and then how would she ever catch her at the moments she was awake?

Cath glanced around the empty room. Every surface was cleared, and except for the bed and a single dresser, there was no other furniture. On a swing arm attached to the bed, used for serving meals, sat a single letter. The return address didn't even give an individual's name but read simply "The Relief Society." The postmark was four months old. Cath couldn't resist and gently pulled the black and white copy of the *Ensign* message out of the envelope. There was no personal note anywhere. Cath dropped the paper on the floor and turned around, engulfed in her own loneliness, coupled with the loneliness of the sleeping woman beside her. She could not let this happen. She couldn't let this poor woman be totally forgotten and ignored by the rest of the world. There had to be a reason Gwen was still here on this earth, if only as a venue for service. Although no one knew when she would wake up, Gwen *did* wake up. And when she did, there was nothing for her to look forward to—nothing to connect her to the outside world.

Suddenly Cath knew exactly what to do. She would start a letter route, just as she had been told. Stepping into the hall, she asked the young aide for paper and something to write with. The girl brought a thick stack of printer paper and an ice cream bucket filled with crayons.

"Crayons?" Cath asked. "I just want to write her a letter or two."

The aide smacked her gum and tapped her foot impatiently. "Some of the residents like to color. Now, I've got to get dinner started so take it or leave it, 'cause that's all I've got."

With a shrug, Cath awkwardly grasped the bucket and smiled her thanks. "Okay, but her room is going to look like my refrigerator door." Thinking about her fridge made Cath chuckle.

The summer had been long and hard. With the move, money was tight, Kevin was still constantly traveling, and there were no other kids in the neighborhood. Cath had tried her best to keep the children entertained by spending hours at the public pool, the library, and the park, but even then by late afternoon they would often arrive home exhausted with a few empty hours left in the day. Carson and Jordan always ran upstairs to continue their next electronic battle, but little Mike, her four-year-old, loved to create crayon pictures and begged his mom to join him. He would color crayon robots, crayon cars that could fly and transform, and crayon superheroes with magical powers. Even her teenage daughter, Sandra, had played along, drawing brilliant crayon sunsets and crayon models with designer clothes, complete with matching hair and makeup and little crayon hearts lining the edges of each page, filling the corners—everywhere.

It had become a game of sorts, trying to find a place on the once clear stainless steel surface of the refrigerator door to display the next piece of artwork. Just the thought of that silly appliance shingled with the work of sweet, lazy, loving afternoons warmed her heart, a feeling she wanted for Gwen.

Dragging in two chairs and a small table from the hall, Cath excitedly set everything down on the table and began to draw intently. She wasn't the greatest artist in the world, or even close, but she was looking for quantity not quality.

✹ one sentence of hope

Jerri Miller arrived as Cath started on her third page, where she was busily drawing each of her four children. Sandra, the oldest, with her long soft brown hair; Jordan, the tall, gangly twelve-year-old with bright red hair and freckles; serious Carson, who at the age of ten carried all the worry of the world on his shoulders; and little Mike with his fair hair sticking straight up and a huge smile on his face. She was so enthralled in her masterpiece that she didn't even notice Jerri march up behind her and begin to inspect the picture of the four stick figures with their names written below each. Suddenly Jerri broke the silence and asked sternly, "What do you think you're doing?"

Embarrassed, Cath realized how rude she had been and put down the crayon. She stood up, extending her hand in greeting. "Sorry, I'm Cath. I was hoping we could get a majority of the room plastered before I had to leave tonight. I hope you like to draw."

"What are you talking about?" Jerri asked, confused.

"Do you know about Gwen's condition?" Cath asked, looking at her sleeping companion.

"Sure, that's why when you said you had talked with her I had to meet you. You've got a lot of gall—I can say that for you," she

9

answered sharply with her hands on her hips and no intention of sitting down.

Cath nodded, imagining what it must have looked like. "The truth is that when I phoned this afternoon, Gwen was awake and thrilled for visitors. No one told me about her situation until I got here, but I had this idea. It seems as though she wakes up every now and then but no one can predict it. Look around this room. When she does wake up, there is nothing of life or the outside world for her to even know someone cares. Can you imagine how depressing that would be? I thought it might be a good idea if every month we drew pictures for her or wrote little notes. Then when she does wake up, she'll have something to look forward to. Do you want to grab a crayon?"

Jerri cracked a subdued grin and shrugged. "That's not a bad plan." She sat down and picked out a dark blue crayon. "What should I do?" she asked flatly.

"Well, I thought we could start by introducing ourselves, and then each month we could share some small part of what's happening in our lives. It might give her a sort of window to life." Jerri nodded in agreement and began writing quickly in small, neat lines. Apparently, she didn't do pictures.

Cath was just finishing a picture of her crooked new house, complete with crooked trees out front. The man who built it had put in all the floors before the roof, and, as luck would have it, it rained for a week. Cath and her husband, Kevin, had gotten a tremendous deal, and the square footage was incredible, but every floor and door frame was wavy and cock-eyed. Finishing that, she pulled out another paper, where she was planning on showing her sons almost diving into toxic waste. The pond in the backyard was actually an open cesspool, and the boys hadn't known. Cath giggled to herself at the Olympic feat she had accomplished, flopping over the deck railing and dashing across the yard to stop them just in time. Afterward she found her thighs filled with slivers, but at least the boys were okay. Jerri's voice yanked her from her thoughts. "So you have four kids, right? I saw your picture."

"Yup, I'm lucky though. I like them so much it makes it easy. Most parents love their kids, but liking them is another matter. I sometimes watch other families and wonder how they do it, but my children are really fun people to be around. How many do you have?" Cath asked automatically.

"Kirt and I could never have children," Jerri said and started writing more intently.

"He would have made a great dad. Do you work or are you home?" Cath asked, filling in the green fumes rising from the water and the little flies above the pond in her picture.

"I actually have a cleaning business now, but we met in the military. I was his commanding officer."

Cath snapped her head up from what she was doing. "Really? How cool!"

"It was one of the best times in my life. I'm one heck of a shot," Jerri mused.

"My boys would love you. Do you play video games?"

"Kirt won't touch them, but *Medal of Honor* and *Call of Duty* are my favorites."

"My two oldest boys are twelve and ten. They have both those games, and the boys think they are such hot shots at it. Would you consider coming over on Friday night and putting them in their place?" Cath smiled, hoping she wasn't crossing any lines.

Jerri nodded slowly. "Sounds good. You sure they won't mind if they lose?"

"They might, but I'd love it," she said, laughing.

"I'll be there." Jerri put down her crayon and stood up. Cath stood too, and Jerri stuck out her hand. "Thanks, Cath. It was good to meet you. I'll see you Friday." She turned on point and marched from the room. Curious, Cath reached down and flipped her paper around so she could read it. The note was direct, introducing herself and giving information about her cleaning business, down to the phone number. But it was the last line that made Cath smile. *See you next month. Jerri.*

The next two visits went well. One older woman, Dorothy Kelly, had been a member of the ward twenty years earlier when Gwen was coherent, and she remembered her well.

"Everyone loved her." Dorothy stroked Gwen's hair and looked at her lovingly. "She was a school teacher if I remember right, until she began falling asleep. Then they had to let her go. I think she also did something in the Primary, but my memory isn't that good anymore."

From the sound of it, Dorothy hadn't been to church in at least ten years, but the offenses she felt she had suffered were as fresh as if they had happened yesterday. When Cath explained what they were doing, Dorothy agreed to think of something to say if Cath would write it down, since Dorothy's hands weren't that good anymore. Dorothy plopped down in the chair, arranged her faded cotton dress to get comfortable, and began her well-rehearsed litany.

"It all started when those women in Relief Society wouldn't leave well enough alone and had suggested that my little Albert was not valiant. Why, that hurt his feelings. Who would want to come when you weren't appreciated and after you had done so much for them? He worked himself half to death over them church people and no one appreciated it. No wonder he never went to church no more, and that's probably why he ended up in jail too. Heaven knows I was the best mother—it wasn't my fault. No, they were vipers at that ward, vipers." Dorothy smiled. "Except that little curly haired boy that belonged to the first counselor's family; he was a treat, just like my Albert when he was a baby. Ask Gwen if she remembers my Albert. He was a good boy. Did you write that all down just like I said?" Dorothy ordered.

Cath nodded but only wrote down about half of what she

said—the good half. After an hour of dictation, Dorothy had got it all out. Cath showed her what she had written and the older woman barely glanced down at the pages. Cath felt sorry for her and guessed that she probably didn't know how to read very well. Dorothy lumbered to her feet, smiling as though she had just finished a friendly chat, and bid Cath farewell, kissing Gwen's forehead on her way out.

As she turned to go, she added, "Cath, dear, can you just send me a letter next time like you do with Gwen there? That's what they always do. Besides, I can't stand places like this. They give me the creeps."

"That's fine." Cath sighed and Dorothy toddled down the hall.

By nine thirty Cath was finished and began taping the pictures and notes to the mirror and up on the walls. Dorothy's letter was four pages long, and Cath had completed twelve pages by herself, mostly pictures. Cath was a little surprised. It hadn't felt like that much had happened since the move, but apparently there was more there than she had expected. She'd even drawn a picture of Tandy and her jogging around the lake. Tandy looked like a blonde Betty Boop doll, and she had drawn herself to look like Mrs. Potato Head. She'd never claimed to be an artist.

When Cath finished, she looked around the room and smiled. It didn't quite have the volume of her fridge, but it did remind her of a kindergartner's room with happy crayon pictures lining the walls, and at least the mirror was totally covered. Cath picked up the leftover paper and crayons and was turning to leave when the nurse from the front desk walked by.

"Visiting hours are over," Sonja stated from the hallway. Peeking in the room curiously, she added, "Looks like you've been busy."

Cath nodded contentedly. "I'll be back Tuesday if that's okay." Sonja had stepped in the room and was carefully eyeing all the papers on the wall. "It will give her something to look at when she wakes up," Cath explained.

The nurse was slowly bobbing her head up and down. "That's nice—real nice." She took the crayons and paper and watched Cath walk away, not moving until she was out of sight. As Cath opened her van door, she remembered Sonja's words. *The best revenge is success.* But she didn't feel vengeful at all; she just felt happy.

❋ a fact-finding mission

With the onset of August, it was almost time to enroll the children in school. The wonderful freedom of summer was eking away. Cath had started scheduling mommy-kid dates, where each child would have a special day to go shopping, update their wardrobe, buy school supplies, and be treated like royalty. She loved that time of year, and even the boys looked forward to it. She also began considering what she would do come fall. Mike, her youngest, was four but would be bored out of his mind at home by himself. Cath had done Joy School a number of times with her other children, but she had called several mothers in the ward and been turned down flat—preschool seemed like a good option for him. Besides, she thought, she could use the time to get in shape at the YMCA or have some leisurely library time. So that was her plan for this afternoon—to check out the Lutheran preschool.

The Central Lutheran Church was massive. That was the only word for it. When they had first arrived in the town of Carson, her ten-year-old had said it looked like a Gothic castle, and he was right. Cath had heard from a grocery store clerk and from one of her new neighbors that this was the best preschool in town and everyone went there whether they were Lutheran or not. When she had called last week, they told her that she needed to apply first, and then Mike would be evaluated. Depending on his performance, he may be put on a waiting list.

Since Cath was not very hopeful that it was even a possibility, she didn't worry about getting dressed up for the occasion. She had left Mike at home with the older children, not wanting to get his hopes up, but standing in front of the massive stone edifice, she was rethinking her decision. It would have been nice to have the moral support. Walking into the grand front hall in sweats (she was planning on checking out the YMCA next), Cath immediately felt like someone in jeans during sacrament meeting. A dozen mothers sat in neat suits with their little sons, combed and pressed, next to them in the long front hallway. As she moved down the imposing gauntlet to the little table at the end of the hall, a college student sat checking off names. Nervously approaching the table, Cath introduced herself. Surprisingly, the girl nodded and told her to go right in. She couldn't believe it, but the girl just motioned to her with her pencil to go through the door at the end of the hall. Cath stepped into the large room, closing the door behind her.

The office was beautiful, with rich mahogany paneling and a stone floor. It even smelled like an old castle and had a fireplace that took up half of the back wall. A large tapestry of Christ at the helm of a raging vessel, holding his hands to the sky, was displayed on the wall. In front of the grand tapestry sat a woman writing quickly at a large clean desk. Cath suddenly felt extremely unsure of herself, like she was standing before a judgment seat, and she softly repeated to herself the words displayed below the tapestry, "Peace, be still." Sitting in one of the two wingback chairs, she waited until the woman behind the desk was done.

Cath watched the wiry woman in her late thirties sit totally absorbed in her paperwork. Her brow was furrowed and her brown frizzy hair wouldn't stay back in her simple bun. She looked so burdened and worried. It wasn't even noon, and Cath thought it looked like she had been working straight through the night. Her reading glasses had slipped down on her nose. "Just one more minute," she said, finishing her scribbling. Then she closed the folder, opened the drawer beside her, and dropped the folder precisely in place. "You are?" she said without looking up.

"Cath Reed. Catherine, that is. My son is Mike, Mike Reed, but I only called a few days ago."

Finding the file, the woman looked up and took off her glasses. "Oh, don't let those ladies in the hall get to you. It's almost lunchtime. From ten thirty to one every day we get our little posse of working mothers who want us to provide full day care. We believe that for children under the age of nine that is best done in the home. We do provide full-time care for a small number of our congregation that are single mothers or whose husbands are disabled, but we are committed not to increase it. Still, they wait, hoping to get in. You are another matter, however. It says here that you are a mother of four?" Cath nodded. "And Mike is your youngest? My question is, why do you want him to be with us?"

"Well, I'm not sure I do. I'm really just here to see if this would be a good fit for him. There aren't any other children his age in the neighborhood, and I want him to have a little bit of social interaction, just a few mornings a week. I'd prefer a home-based preschool but haven't been able to find other mothers willing to do it with me. You were the next best option."

"Really? That is the most refreshing thing I've heard in months. I'm Pattie Wilson." She stood, and a light shone from her eyes that hadn't been there before. Cath couldn't help but smile as she shook her hand. "Would you like to come and look at our facility?"

"Thanks." Cath was surprised when Pattie stood and walked to a small door behind her that looked like a closet. It led down a narrow winding stone staircase to a dark basement hall. Looking at the cold stone walls, Cath felt like she was about to enter an evil dungeon. She was beginning to think she might pass on this whole idea when Pattie opened two gray metal doors. It was like that part of the *Wizard of Oz* where everything turns to color. Three large pillars stood evenly across a huge sunny room. They had been wrapped with some sort of rubberized fake tree bark, spreading to fake branches and silk green leaves on the ceiling. The massive open room had different play stations reflecting each area of a home. The kitchen had play utensils and fake food with oven mitts and aprons, where little girls were busy pretending to serve delicious meals. Another corner of the room had about ten small rocking chairs and one big one. A few children sat in their little rocking chairs listening to an older woman gently read *Are You My Mother?* about a little bird who gets lost—one of Cath's favorites.

Another area had big bouncy balls with handles, and little scooters. The children would lie on their tummies on the scooters and push around the floor with their hands and legs. A little picket fence kept the rowdy boys in check as they rolled around, bounced, and played. There was an art area with smocks, easels, and modeling clay. Lastly, a large indoor playground spanned the width of the entire back of the basement. It seemed to have been excavated after the church was built and extended beyond the cathedral's foundation so that the ceiling was glass, letting the sunshine fill the entire space. It was magical.

"Pattie," Cath turned to her, "this is incredible. What a marvelous place."

Pattie shook her head, discouraged. "I really pushed for this school as a way to help full-time mothers stay home. I thought if they could have a break while they did their shopping or even just took a few extra hours a week to themselves that they would be more willing to give up the things of the world for their children and have more energy to offer them. Instead, every year more and more mothers are leaving their children to go to work unnecessarily, and we get more and more pressure from the church leaders to increase our profits and accept full-time day care. I'm wondering if all I have done is encourage the very thing I was trying stop."

Cath wanted to throw her arms around this kindred spirit. She felt like finally there was someone here that felt the way she did about so many things. "Wow, you did all this?"

Pattie nodded. "I've gone to this church my whole life, and, believe it or not, I was an art and design major." Looking at the unique indoor playground and the cute wooden cut-outs around the walls, painted with bright colors and the trees, Cath could completely believe it. "When Mr. Right never came along, this became my life's work. Mrs. Reed, it is women like you that I made this resource for, and we would be honored to have your son Mike come play with us."

"I think he would love it, but I worry that three mornings a week is too much. Could he just come Tuesdays and Thursdays? I don't think I'm ready to lose him for three days quite yet." Pattie smiled, and they went upstairs to finish the paperwork. As she left the office, Cath felt like she was walking on air. Finally, she had found the hope of a true friend.

With her hand on the huge door, ready to return to her car, Cath suddenly stopped. A muffled sound drew her back inside and down an opulent hallway like a child after the Pied Piper. The sound became louder, and she pushed open the two large doors and was immediately enveloped by the powerful vibrations of a complex organ number. The chapel, or sanctuary as they referred to it, reminded her of a square Mormon Tabernacle. Gleaming pipes filled the room, blasting, flowing, and twirling around the room. The organist sat at his instrument with his feet moving like he was dancing while his hands hopped from one keyboard to another with practiced ease. The complexity of his music was hypnotic, and Cath slowly found herself walking up the aisle, drawn closer to the intricate harmonies. It was awe-inspiring.

As the number finished, Cath stood there awkwardly, suddenly feeling like an intruder, and turned to leave. The organist called out cheerily, "What did you think? Any requests?"

"It was gorgeous," she stammered. "Just incredible."

"If you think this organ sounds good, you should hear the one in the Mormon church building," the petite man said, putting away his music and walking toward her with quick staccato steps. "It was Dan Barton's magnum opus, a true masterpiece. Such a clear voice—I really miss it." He was a slender and tidy man who stood just over five feet tall with dark rim glasses. He wore a plain suit with a white shirt and thin black tie. It was hard to tell if he was decades out of fashion or on the cutting edge of it. Cath guessed that he had dressed the same way his entire life and didn't really care what the world thought.

As he stepped down the aisle, she noticed his shoes were freshly polished. People who worried about those sort of details always made her nervous because her details were never taken care of, and she started becoming more uncomfortable with the fact that she was still wearing sweats and hadn't showered yet that morning. He looked at her appraisingly with intelligent, analytical eyes, and she felt compelled to say something.

"I'm a Mormon," she blurted out. "And that small organ at our church doesn't seem like anything compared to this." She held up her hands and looked around. Pipes filled the back of the hall and danced up and down both sides of the chapel, ending with the grandest display at the front of the room.

The organist shook his head. "Looks can be deceiving. An organ should be custom designed to respect the musical, architectural, and acoustical space of its environment. Dan Barton was a master of that. The old organ was an original, designed specifically for this building by the greatest organ builder in history. These new pop-up companies have lost the art of creating a true instrument—they're all show. Do you see the pretty little pipes up and down the sides of the sanctuary? Their sounds are lost in the rafters. If you ever use them, it's a waste of energy just pushing the stops. Those pipes in the back, which should be the strong bass notes booming from behind, are treble notes, and the bass sit in the front, overwhelming all the other subtle sounds, making everything you play sound like oatmeal."

"It sounded beautiful to me," Cath said.

"You're a Mormon. Haven't you heard that instrument played? Can't you tell the difference?" She couldn't bear to tell him about their organist, Wanda Witherby. The little woman who played the organ on Sunday looked like a five-year-old driving a Cadillac. Cath doubted the woman could even reach the foot pedals if she tried, which was just as well because half the notes she played were incorrect.

"Just so you understand the value of what you have, let me explain. Dan Barton was an organ maker who started his craft across the river right at the turn of the century. He originally became famous building theatre organs during the vaudeville and silent movie eras. He focused on compact organs with rich, vibrant tones. The secret was in the pipes—a secret he never shared. In the late twenties, with the onset of the talking film, Dan Barton turned to churches. He built fewer than twenty church organs before his death, but each is a veritable masterpiece. That is the organ that sits in your chapel, while we are stuck with a Wal-Mart special."

"Why did your leaders ever agree to part with it?" she asked, astonished.

He put a hand to his chin and pointed with his other. Cath could tell he had completely analyzed the situation, but understanding it had not made it any easier for him to deal with. "Two driving factors led the committee to this foolhardy decision. First, they were hoping the publicity of a new organ would increase membership, and second, a large donation encouraged the waffling board members to bend their decisions. It paid for the new one with a considerable sum remaining. It was simply coincidence that all this happened just at the time the new Mormon church was being built. By donating it, the board could claim its value to be much more than they would ever get on the open market, and so it was done. The saddest part is that they never even recognized the treasure within their grasp and without that understanding threw away something truly precious."

"Unfortunately that happens far too often in this world," Cath said, thinking of her recent discussion with Pattie and of Gwen alone in her empty room. Snapping back to reality, she extended her hand. "Sorry, I'm Cath Reed. I was just enrolling my youngest son in preschool. I better get home to the kids—it's Sandra's mommy date day and I'm stealing her time. Thank you for your wonderful music; it just lifted me."

"Oh," the organist replied slowly, "Ralph Beckman. You are welcome to come and listen any time you wish. I come every Tuesday at this time, for the exercise." He looked at her with raised eyebrows, laughing at his own joke, and Cath suddenly became self-conscious of her sweats again.

"It was nice to meet you," Cath said and turned awkwardly, leaving the room and going outside. *What a brilliant, talented, and interesting organist*, she thought. How she wished she could learn to play like that. And what a surprise to think that her ward had this wonderful hidden treasure right in their chapel that they weren't even using to its greatest potential. The words caught in her brain as if displayed on a billboard. She wondered how many other untapped treasures in the gospel were just like that—the scriptures, prayer, and temple attendance—being underused when they had the ability to transform life into beauty.

It was after one when Cath pulled up the driveway to see Sandra pacing anxiously on the front porch. Her beautiful fourteen-year-old daughter ran up to the passenger door and jumped in. "Mom, where have you been? What were you doing all morning? All my friends are meeting at the mall, and I'm late."

"Wait. I thought this would be our time together. What friends? Do I know them?"

Sandra rolled her eyes and clicked her tongue in disgust. "Oh, Mom, they're all members of the Church, so stop worrying. You just have to drop me off. I'll even use my own money. Sister Jacobs said she'll give me a ride home."

"Why isn't Jordan going? Are there going to be kids his age there too?" Cath asked on the verge of giving in.

"Jordan is with Carson in the bonus room killing aliens. Please, Mom. I'm late."

As Cath put the car in gear to take Sandra to meet her new friends, she found her stomach knotting. It had been such an odd day filled with unexpected things. First the preschool, then the organist, and then losing this mommy date with no warning—but Cath supposed it was normal for her daughter to grow out of these kind of experiences. She glanced at Sandra, who was staring in the visor mirror putting on lipstick, and she felt so far away from her.

✳ are we having fun yet?

At six thirty on Friday evening, Kevin walked through the door and could hear his wife yelling at the kids, "Get up right now and finish that vacuuming. The Millers will be here any second, and I still have to mop the kitchen floor. Mike, pick up that blanket and bring it to your room right now. The next person to make a mess in this house will be locked in one of the cars!"

Stomping down the stairs into the kitchen, she found Kevin sitting on one of the new swivel oak stools at the counter. Like a kid at a soda fountain, he was swinging back and forth, back and forth, calmly. He smiled at her quizzically. "Having fun yet?"

"Fun? I've got so much to do, you can't even imagine. I spent the whole day cleaning while Mike and Carson spent the time making a secret potion out of every shampoo and lotion bottle in our bathroom. It was a disaster. So while I'm cleaning that up, the kids go back into the playroom and yank out all the videos I had just put away. I can't stay ahead of them. It is driving me batty."

"Well," said Kevin softly, "let it go and speak a little more softly because I think the Millers are here." Cath looked around the kitchen, which still had a sticky floor, crumbs on the island, and grocery bags on the counter, and took a deep breath, trying to take her husband's advice—it was time to have fun.

Kevin ran to the door and threw it open as the older boys bounded down the stairs. Despite herself, Cath grabbed a rag and swiftly wiped down the kitchen, hurrying into the front hall before she was missed. She shook hands with Jerri and Bishop Miller, not realizing her hands were wet until it was too late. Jordan and Carson had been developing strategies for the last five days and were chomping at the bit to pit their military prowess against a real marine. Jordan got behind the bishop's wife, and Carson was at the front asking details of her background and trying to draw her upstairs.

"Do you like an M16 better or a P90?"

"Have you been trained in martial arts? Can you show us some of your best moves?" Jordan added.

Bishop Miller and Kevin veered to the left and entered the office while the kids and Jerri headed upstairs to the bonus room. They were two-thirds of the way there when the doorbell rang again. Cath opened the door to a teenage boy dressed in a white T-shirt and jeans, but rather than looking sloppy, he reminded her of a young James Dean.

"Jordan and Carson said you guys were playing games tonight and asked me to come," the boy said.

Cath was impressed and welcomed him in, happy that Jordan was finally making friends, when Sandra came running down the stairs. Sandra was wearing tight jeans and a sequined tube top made semi-modest by a thin bolero jacket. It was the first Cath had seen of the outfit, which her daughter must have picked up at the mall the other day. Her eye makeup was heavy, and Cath couldn't believe how old it made her young daughter look. "Hi, Zee. Everyone is upstairs."

She grabbed his arm and tried to slip past her mother as quickly as possible, but Cath stepped right in front of them and smiled that smile that does not quite reach her eyes. She stared at her daughter and then at the boy next to her. "Zee, I don't think we have officially met. You look familiar; do I know you from somewhere?"

Sandra glared at her mother angrily, but Cath waited patiently for the boy's reply. "I'm Zeniff Jacobs. You know my mom, Hillary. People just call me Zee, 'cause it sounds cool." He grinned as though he had just said the smartest thing in the world, and Sandra looked up at him admiringly.

"Zeniff. That's from the Book of Mormon, isn't it?" Cath asked.

Sandra stepped forward and lifted her nose. "Everyone in their family has Book of Mormon names. His brother is Corianton—he goes by Cory—and his sister is TeaAnn."

"TeaAnn?" Cath asked. "I don't remember that name from the scriptures."

"Well," said Zee patronizingly, "my parents didn't like any of the girls' names so they figured when they called her they would say, 'TeaAnn, come.' Get it? Teancum?" Sandra laughed a little too hard at the joke and stared in Zee's eyes. Cath felt that uneasiness in the pit of her stomach return but wasn't sure how best to handle the obvious crush developing before her eyes. She stepped aside and allowed them to pass, determined to get upstairs as soon as possible.

As they left, Cath realized why she had felt so uncomfortable. She chided herself for not figuring out that Sandra had invited Zee. Dashing back into the kitchen, she began to organize the toppings for the sundaes as quickly as she could so she could get upstairs, when the doorbell rang again. Cath couldn't imagine who it could be, but the short, stocky image through the beveled glass was unmistakable. *What could Lynnette want?* she thought.

Tuesday night at the nursing home had been nice. She had written to Gwen about her plans for tonight, the wonderful preschool she had found for Mike, and the organ, adding another six pictures. As she was taping the pictures to the wall, the quiet of the room was suddenly shattered by two arguing children running at full speed down the hall. Cath was just feeling a little annoyed by their unchecked commotion when they burst into Gwen's room, followed by their mother.

Lynnette was a single mom who had stopped all association with the Church when she felt socially abandoned by the ward after her divorce. She claimed it had been a public humiliation, and she just couldn't face anyone she knew. But after chatting with her for a while, Cath found that Lynnette was well aware of all the latest callings and knew more about what was going on in the ward than she did. When Cath told her about Gwen, Lynnette had said she couldn't come because of her children, but Cath thought it would be great to bring them along. Now she was beginning to doubt it. The entire visit was exhausting, what with trying to keep the two out-of-control twins from destroying everything Cath had tried to do. They yanked pictures off the walls and even ripped a few. Cath gave them each a chair and encouraged the eight-year-old brother and sister to make their own pictures for Gwen, but they said she looked dead and just scribbled and broke the crayons. Cath tried to be gracious but was secretly happy when the visit was over.

As she opened the door, Lynnette stood smiling sweetly on the porch with her children buzzing around her. As soon as they saw the opening, they whizzed past Cath and scattered. "So are you having a party?" Lynnette asked hopefully. "The Millers' and the Jacobs's cars are outside. I saw them."

"Oh, it's nothing. The kids are just upstairs with Sister Miller playing video games; it's only . . ." Before she could finish speaking, Lynnette squeezed past Cath and was halfway up the stairs, feigning the need to chase after one of her children. "Winnette, we probably should go now," she called weakly, continuing forward. Cath followed after her, trying again to take her husband's advice and just let it go.

As they walked down the hall to the bonus room, Cath caught sight of the children's rooms and cringed. Winlyn was nowhere to be seen, but his trail of destruction was obvious: the Lego bins in Mike and Carson's room had been dumped out, and a number of action figures had their arms ripped off. Winnette was in Sandra's room alone, jumping on the bed. She knew Sandra would be furious but figured she could deal with it later and continued following Lynnette to the bonus room.

The room was wall to wall people. Jerri Miller was given the place of honor at the center of the couch, directly in front of the TV, and was clicking away at her controller with calm precision. Jordan had a controller too and was making all sorts of faces, a clear sign he was in way over his head. Carson was squeezed in beside him shouting commands while wildly flipping around and thwacking his thumbs. On the other side of Jerri, Zee was tapping at his controller with confidence and seemed to be holding his own. Next to him sat Sandra, and Cath's mouth fell open. Her daughter had her arm looped in his and was batting her eyelashes in his direction. Just then Carson yelled, "Zee, you just killed one of your own men again. Are you color-blind?"

"Hey, stop picking on Zee," shouted Sandra. "He's doing great!" Zee smiled at Sandra, who glowed back at him.

Jordan sneered. "If losing is great, then have at it, Zee."

Winlyn and Mike were jumping up and down behind the couch, calling out commands randomly. "Dodge! Shoot! Go left!"

Lynnette stared at the group with her hands on her hips for a second, hoping to be noticed, and then walked right in front of the TV, staring closely at the screen. "What are you guys watching?" she asked. Instantly everyone craned their necks around her or scooted over so they could see the screen.

"Move!" commanded Jerri.

"We can't see, Sister Young!" Carson called, trying to be polite, but somewhat annoyed.

"Mom, move your big fat butt!" shouted Winlyn.

Lynnette would not move and looked closer at the screen. "Are you shooting people? Are you practicing killing each other?" she asked indignantly.

Cath couldn't stand it anymore. This was her house, and she would not let Lynnette ruin her family's evening. Trying to save the situation from imploding, she asked, "Lynnette, could you please help me downstairs? We're going to have banana splits in a few minutes and we would love for your family to join us." Without waiting for a reply, Cath linked her arm in the other woman's and began walking. Lynnette had no choice but to follow. Cath continued talking. "Are your children allergic to nuts?"

Leaping at the bait, Lynnette found something new to whine about and began listing the many foods that each one of her twins couldn't or wouldn't eat. Nuts were not on the list. They were in the middle of the staircase when Cath saw Winnette running across the front hall with her Steuben glass crystal apple. It was an heirloom from her grandmother. Cath dropped Lynnette's arm and bolted forward, catching the little imp before she made it into the back room.

Taking away the treasure, Cath couldn't believe it when Winnette stuck out her tongue, kicked her in the shins, and ran upstairs. Her mother had been standing right beside her, doing nothing. Cath put the crystal on top of the refrigerator while behind her Lynnette was busily rifling through the bags of groceries still out on the counter. "I don't see any Magic Shell. That's Winnette's favorite. Didn't you buy any Magic Shell?"

Cath grabbed the bananas, a bowl, and a knife and put them in front of her. "Why don't you cut up the bananas and I'll get out the bowls and utensils?" she suggested, her patience growing thin.

"They must be cut unpeeled so they don't turn brown. That is the only way to do it," Lynnette commanded.

"That will be fine, whatever you choose." Cath put a large stack of bowls and spoons on the island. Then she quickly dumped the nuts in a bowl and opened the cherries, caramel, and pineapple toppings. She was just about to warm the hot fudge when Carson clomped down the stairs in a huff.

"Mom, Zee and Sandra are driving me crazy. It is just gross to watch, and Winlyn is destroying everything. All he wants to do is rip things apart. He has yanked every arm off our action figures and is now trying to chop off the big Mutant Ninja Turtle's head."

At that moment a huge crash reverberated from the back room. If Cath wanted to salvage this night, she knew it was time to act. "Lynnette," she ordered, "please go take care of Winnette. I'll run upstairs and call the other children. Carson, you microwave the hot fudge. I'll be right back."

Dashing up the stairs, she stuck her head into the boys' room. Winlyn was twisting and pulling at the head of the twelve-inch plastic turtle action figure. She walked over to him and yanked poor Raphael away. "Winlyn, we will be having treats downstairs. Hurry or you won't get any." He ran off, and Cath looked at the disaster around her. Carson had not been exaggerating.

Mike shook his head. "It wasn't me, Mom, I promise."

In Sandra's room, the bed was totally stripped of its sheets and the closet was half empty, her new school clothes scattered all over the floor. Cath knew that a big blowout was coming from both sides of the spectrum. She looked down and shook her head at a halter top and mini-skirt that still had the tags on. Sandra had never done anything like this before. At least they could still be returned—and they would be.

Going into the bonus room, she had the worst surprise yet. Jerri and Jordan were still deeply entrenched in their battle, but Zee had abandoned his game for something more interesting. Sandra was almost sitting on his lap. Cath watched silently at the door while Sandra touched his face and stared in his eyes. "I never realized your eyes were so green, Zee. Do you know what green eyes mean?"

Every muscle in Cath's body tightened as she ran forward and stood beside the TV, shouting like a crazy woman, "Can you pause this, please? We are having sundaes downstairs and then you can come back and play as late as you like." It took all of her self-control not to yank her daughter into the other room, but Cath felt sure that now was not the time to discuss it. The only thing that allowed her to turn her back and wait for the kids to follow was the sure knowledge she had that when the kids went back upstairs to play, Zee would not be with them. She wasn't sure how, but she prayed that somehow she could make it happen.

As she reentered the kitchen, people were streaming in, and Cath noticed that there were still three minutes left on the microwave timer, but the hot fudge inside was bubbling away like crazy. "Carson, what time did you put that on?"

"Ten minutes," he answered, dishing up his ice cream.

Cath called frantically to her husband, who was standing right by the microwave, "Pull that hot fudge out of the microwave this instant. It's going to burn, Kevin."

Without thinking, Kevin opened the microwave door and reached his hand in to grab the bottle. The scalding syrup, which had oozed over the side, immediately fused to his flesh. He whooped once and dropped it on the island, dashing over to the faucet to run his injured hand under cold water. Carson was standing beside him and quickly righted the jar, but not before a big blob of hot chocolate sauce had flopped on the counter. Seconds later, Winnette wiggled up onto the stool beside it and dipped her finger in the burning-hot goo. Suddenly it was as though all the fire alarms in the house had gone off simultaneously.

"Aaaah! My hand is on fire! It burns! I'm dying! I'm dying!" Winnette screamed with all her might. "Aaaaaah!" Her face

31

turned bright red, and Cath was amazed by the extreme drama of her behavior.

Lynnette rushed to her daughter's side. "Oh, honey, are you okay?"

Her mother's question seemed to fuel the fire, and the child's screams intensified. "My finger is going to fall off. It's burnt to the bone. I'm dying!" The little girl was shaking as if she were in shock. Cath couldn't believe her eyes. She calmly walked over with a rag to wipe off her finger, but Lynnette stood in front of the girl with her arms out wide.

"I was a nurse. If that burn is serious, it could take off the skin. Winlyn, get in the car! We're going to the hospital!" She had a frantic look in her eye, and Cath could tell the woman was totally losing it. Even Lynnette's children seemed to know the writing on the wall, and the two whirlwinds zipped out of the house as quickly as they had come in.

Their minivan roared away, and the entire room was just letting out a sigh of relief as Zee and Sandra finally made their way into the kitchen, totally oblivious to what had just happened. Zee stepped forward and sat on Winnette's empty stool.

"Oh, hot fudge," he said nonchalantly and stuck his finger in the still-boiling mixture. His quick football reflexes realized his error. He pulled back his chocolate-covered finger and quickly shook off the offending mess, which flung over and landed squarely on Sandra's new tube top.

Embarrassed, she grabbed a dish rag and started trying to clean it off, smearing it all over the front of her. Zee laughed, and she glared at him angrily. "You—you, big klutz! Look at my new shirt."

"What are you talking about? I'm the one who burned my finger. I'm out of here." Zee marched out the kitchen door and slammed it behind him. Sandra looked around for someone to blame and then threw up her hands and ran from the room crying.

As Cath heard Zee's car peel out and plow down the driveway, she shook her head, wishing it were only that easy. No, Cath had a feeling she would see Zee again far too soon, and she worried she might lose her daughter in the process.

It was Jerri who broke the silence that followed, "Well, Carson, I'm proud of you. You found a great use for hot fudge."

❋ cleaning up messes

The rest of the night really was fun, at least for everyone else. The *Call of Duty* crowd went upstairs again and was still going strong. Cath watched for a while, long enough to realize how good Jerri was. She was a master, but she used her talents to train the boys, not to beat them. They would even replay big blunders so they knew how not to be caught with their pants down. It really was a military simulation the way Jerri played it.

Finally Cath wandered down the hall and took a deep breath. It was time to face her daughter. She knocked softly and stuck her head in. Sandra was lying across the bare mattress with her head in her pillow, not moving.

"Sweetie, are you awake?"

"No," the muffled answer came with Sandra not even lifting her head from the pillow.

"Can we talk?" Cath sat on the edge of her daughter's bed and touched her gently.

Sandra flipped over on her back and hugged her knees in a fluid motion. "Mom, you don't want to talk; you want to lecture me. You want to rub salt in my open wounds. It's just that no one ever liked me before, not that way." She started to cry again but shook her head and tried to continue. "Do you even get it? Zee is the most popular guy in this high school. You can't understand what just happened. I have been branded for life. When I start high school, I'll be blacklisted. My life is over."

Tears streamed down her daughter's face and Cath looked at her sympathetically. All the things she had planned on saying about being wary of relationships at her age, dressing immodestly, and— worst of all—hiding things from her mother, seemed to go out the window for now. She reached out to comfort her sweet little girl. "Sandra, I'm so sorry this happened, but maybe it was for the best."

"The best?" Sandra pulled away from her mother and looked at her like the enemy. "For the best? How could you say such a thing? I hate you. I am never going to speak to you again." Sandra threw her face back in the pillow, and Cath sat quietly beside her for a few more minutes. From the time she was a toddler, Sandra had a will of stone, and Cath knew from experience that it would take time before Sandra would be ready to open up. Cath would give her that space, but in the meantime she would watch her like a hawk. Closing Sandra's door behind her, Cath made her way to the office to join the men. They were talking sports, and after they mentioned the fourth athlete Cath had never heard of, she went back to the kitchen to pull it together.

The hot fudge had cooled and lay in a hardened mass on the counter. Bowls and spoons and drippy empty ice cream cartons littered the room, dusted with chopped nuts like confetti. She began scrubbing vigorously and tossing dishes in the sink. With her hands busy, Cath's mind was free to wander. This Sandra thing was a whole new chapter that she and Kevin hadn't thought they would have to face quite yet. Cath was suddenly struck with a strong desire to phone her mother and ask for advice, but just as suddenly her heart deflated. It had been two years since her mom had unexpectedly passed away, and the dull ache would always be there. But at times like this, her death seemed as poignant as if it were yesterday. Her father was still alive, but he wouldn't understand. He would tell her to force Sandra to toe the line. No, she just wanted to talk to her mother—to get a clean perspective and be loved. Cath's loneliness enveloped her, and she had to leave the kitchen and find someone to hug.

It was almost eleven when she walked up to Mike's room to tuck him in. When she saw him, her heart sank. Her youngest son was slumped over a pile of Lego's, fast asleep. Apparently he had started to clean them up—the bin next to him was almost half full—but had zonked out in the middle of the job. She lifted her boy up to put him in his bed, three of the plastic pieces still stuck to his cheek. Laying him down, she smoothed his angel soft hair, kissed his cheek, and then decided to cuddle up next to him, planning to close her eyes for only a second.

The next morning she woke up in Mike and Carson's room alone. Cath got up and walked into the master bedroom to find the boys snuggled up with their dad, who was still snoring loudly. She brushed her teeth and changed her clothes. It was eight in the morning, and she wanted to run over to the nursing home before the family got up and deliver the flowers she had bought yesterday for Gwen's room. When she kissed Kevin's forehead, his eyes shot open. "Where are you going?"

"I'll be right back," Cath whispered. "How long did the Millers stay?"

"They left around two in the morning, I think. Jerri would have stayed longer, but Bishop Miller had to work. When will you be home?"

"I should be back in an hour. I'll grab something for breakfast."

Ten minutes later Cath was driving up to the Pleasant Valley Home for the Elderly. She was thinking she might draw a picture about the lethal hot fudge incident. It might make Gwen laugh, and perhaps Gwen would have some ideas of how to deal with Sandra. As she walked up to the glass partition with a huge pot of flowers in her arms, the burly nurse smiled. "I've got something for you," she beamed happily. Cath almost wondered if this was the same person she had first met.

After rummaging through a pile of letters, Sonja handed her one. "Gwen woke up yesterday. I told her what you did and she wanted to write everybody letters. I haven't seen her that happy—ever. She stayed awake for over two hours. It was a miracle." There were tears glistening in Sonja's eyes, and Cath was speechless.

Sonja buzzed her through and Cath grabbed the envelope. "Thank you," she said and walked down the hall, still a little dazed. When she got to Gwen's room, Cath was amazed. It was filled with almost twice as many pictures and notes as she had left the last time she was there. Many were from people she didn't even know. Putting down the flowers, Cath pulled up a chair right next to Gwen. Her beautiful face almost shone, and Cath held her soft hand as she read her words, hoping that somehow she would feel a connection to her.

Gwen's handwriting was impeccable; every letter was formed perfectly with generous flourishes.

Dear Cath,

Sonja has told me what you did for me. I recall talking to you and was looking forward to meeting you—and now I have. I love your pictures and notes. They make me smile and want to live. I can tell that you have a kind and generous heart. But one thing worries me. Your children seem so happy, but you don't. Did you notice that every picture you drew was of something you were upset about? A crooked house, a cesspool, a fat self-portrait that I'm guessing isn't very accurate. When you look at me, Cath, think of how short this life is. You're doing so many good things, but you need to enjoy it more. Can you do just one favor for me? Have fun. Do something that makes you feel totally happy, and then tell me about it. I can't wait to hear what it is.

Love, Gwen

Cath let go of Gwen's hand and stared at the page, and then stared at the woman beside her. Gwen was challenging her. She was giving her a homework assignment. Cath hardly knew what to do, it was so unexpected. But how difficult could it be? She put the letter in her purse, determined to take on this challenge. Within the week she promised herself that she would be back with her report and it would be the most fun anyone had ever had in their entire life, whether it killed her or not.

✹ the silent treatment

The Sunday after receiving Gwen's letter, Cath was still looking for something fun to report on. Unfortunately, the rest of Saturday was spent recovering from Friday night, and there was no time for fun of any kind. The big crash she had heard in the back room had been her floor lamp joining a massive pile of items, many of which she didn't even know she owned and now weren't worth keeping. Winnette was a very determined child, if nothing else. At least Sunday morning had gone extremely well despite the fact that Kevin had to leave on another business trip. He was balancing an overload of clients, and the promise that he would be home every weekend was dwindling to getting home late Friday night and leaving first thing Sunday morning so he would be fresh for his Monday morning meetings. Still, all the children had laid out their Sunday clothes and bathed the night before, so they made it to the car without a single sock hunt or wrinkled shirt. For her family, that was a minor miracle, but she didn't think Gwen would count it as fun.

Pulling into the parking lot, Cath noticed Tandy Kates arrive at the same time. As she approached the front door, Tandy put a gentle hand on Cath's shoulder. Cath slowed and turned to smile at her, thinking she was finally going to speak to her again and maybe laugh about their jogging experience. Tandy leaned forward and whispered loudly in Cath's ear, "Cathy, your skirt has a slit. I thought you knew how immodest that is, and totally inappropriate for church. You'll have to go get a safety pin out of the library before someone sees you."

Cath looked down at her long khaki skirt that went almost to her ankles. The slit stopped three inches below her knees so that she could walk. She wore a white collared shirt beneath a lightweight cotton sweater. Then she looked at Tandy, who was wearing a skin-tight black wraparound dress made of thin polyester that showed off every curve and dimple of her perfect figure. It stopped above her knees, except where it wrapped in front, which opened with each step to reveal the black lace hem of her expensive slip. A part of Cath wanted to point to her and ask if she considered that to be a slit, but she just smiled and whispered, "Good morning," while continuing moving forward with the children. Sandra giggled and then turned from her mother, still giving her the silent treatment since Friday night.

Once in their seats, Cath listened to the prelude and tried to put the experience from her mind, focusing on the golden voice of Dan Barton's masterpiece. She was enjoying being the only one to know the secret about this hidden treasure and for some reason wasn't anxious to share it. The clear tones of "I Am a Child of God" did sound wonderful, like a high-quality flute, but Cath really wanted to try it out for herself. She was definitely not a great pianist and had never attempted the organ, but she could do a pretty decent job accompanying Primary or Relief Society without embarrassing herself. A part of Cath that she never knew existed before wanted to flood the room with the beauty she had heard from Ralph Beckman, but she doubted that she would ever get the opportunity and put the thought behind her like some silly dream.

When sacrament meeting ended, Cath rushed Mike to the Primary room and got him settled in his class. As she turned to go, she couldn't believe her eyes. There stood Lynnette. She had told Cath it had been over a year since she had come, but here she was. Cath felt like Friday night might have been worth it after all and approached her with open arms.

"This is yours." Lynnette shoved a $1,500 hospital bill at Cath angrily. "We took Winnette to the emergency room and had to wait for four hours. They said that she had a second degree burn. It had to be professionally wrapped and watched for signs of infection."

"I'm sorry," Cath said sincerely.

"Well," said Lynnette shaking her head emphatically and pointing to the paper in her hand, "sorry won't pay the bills. I can't believe you would have such a dangerous situation with children around. It is just irresponsible."

With that, she spun around and marched into the Primary room. The minute Cath saw Winnette in the hall, she ran over to her. "Oh, sweetie, how is your finger?" she asked, concerned.

Winnette held her unbandaged digit up and stated proudly, "I have a blister, see?"

"I'm so sorry," Cath said, kissing the small injury. She thought of the hot red burn that Kevin still had wrapped in gauze and shook her head slightly. "Well, I hope you have a wonderful day in Primary." As Winnette sauntered away, Cath stood up and looked at the bill in her hand. She thought of the pile of broken things at the bottom of the stairs worth far more than $1,500 and shook her head at the injustice of it all. Suddenly, all the luster of the day had left her and she walked down the hall completely alone. The small clusters of people talking around her did not acknowledge her presence, and she felt as invisible as Gwen. When she stood at the door to the Gospel Doctrine class, she couldn't bear to enter. She had no desire to sit alone in a room full of strangers. No, today she just couldn't do it.

Cath turned and wandered back into the lobby, unsure of what to do next. She couldn't go home because she had to be there to pick up the children. Then she caught sight of the open chapel doors. The large room was empty. She pulled the door closed behind her and walked past the maroon upholstered pews to the front podium, around it, and up the little stairs. The organ was not locked, and she sat down on the bench, feeling rebellious. Pushing the swell pedal up so that it would be as soft as possible, she turned to page 124 in the hymn book. There were three sets of keyboards and various stops all around the organ with different numbers and instruments on them. She chose the strings and pulled out a bunch of them randomly, not really sure what she was doing. Putting the brass beneath, Cath began to play softly,

Be still, my soul: The Lord is on thy side;
With patience bear thy cross of grief or pain.
Leave to thy God to order and provide;
In every change he constant will remain.
Be still my soul: Thy best, thy heav'nly Friend.
Thru thorny ways leads to a joyful end.

The music rang through the room and deep into her heart. As the words silently floated through her mind, Cath knew that somehow she would make it through this. She played with some other stops and tried it again with the foot pedals playing the lowest bass notes. That's when Cath began to get a glimpse of what that organist had said to her. The room reverberated with power even at the softest level. A part of her wanted to blast "The Spirit of God," but she knew it would disturb the classes still in session. Cath was so focused on what she was doing that she never noticed Bishop Miller standing behind her. She jumped when he put his hand on her shoulder. She abruptly stopped and twirled to face him, wondering if he had been in the room the whole time or just barely walked in. Embarrassed, she felt that she had been caught red-handed.

"Keep playing." He smiled, but she quickly stood up.

"No, I'm not very good."

"Sister Reed," he said, looking in her eyes, "I need to thank you for the other night. It meant the world to me and my wife. She hasn't had that much fun in years."

"The boys had a great time too. We'll have to get together again soon. That is all they've been talking about."

"You have a great family," he smiled.

"I know," she said confidently. "They're wonderful."

Then the bishop focused on Cath seriously. "So are you."

She grew embarrassed and looked down. "Well, Lynnette doesn't think so. She just handed me a hospital bill. I know our homeowners insurance will cover it, but . . ."

"Sister Reed, when the Lord told us to let our light shine before men, he did not say that everyone would benefit from it. Have you ever thrown on the light to wake up one of your teenagers for seminary? They cringe, don't they, and maybe even complain a little?"

Cath smiled at the visual. "That's an understatement, but I get the idea."

"You just keep shining and do what you know is right and I'm sure that you will find that many unexpected patches of ground start to blossom like never before. Thank you, Sister Reed. You are a real gift to us."

Cath grew misty at his sincerity and watched the bishop continue down the aisle and out the doors. Maybe things would get better. Kevin would get through this next bout of traveling and in a few months would be home more. Sandra would cool off and come around. And maybe Cath would even invite Pattie out to lunch next time she dropped off Mike. Encouraged, she let out a deep breath, realizing how much better she felt. Throwing caution to the wind, Cath sat back at the bench and flipped to page two, threw back the swell pedal to its loudest, and stumbled her way through the most poorly executed but thoroughly enjoyed rendition of "The Spirit of God" that Dan Barton's organ had ever experienced. It was fun! When she was done, she turned off the organ, almost giggling to herself, and walked up the aisle, assuming it was about time for the meetings to be over.

There, waiting for her at the chapel doors, was Hillary Jacobs with her hands on her hips. As she approached her, Cath could see the look of frustration on her face and wondered how she could have offended her. Was she upset about Zee's finger too?

"I am very concerned about the environment you are exposing my young son to. I have it on good authority that recently he was at your house while M-rated video games were being played. That is the same as R-rated movies. I will choose to believe that you were simply ignorant of the standards of the Church and that I will never have to have this discussion with you again in the future."

"Hillary, I don't know where you heard that, but the games the boys were playing were rated T for Teen. Do you want me to bring the jackets so you can see for yourself?" Cath asked calmly.

"I don't care what you say—they were M. I have documented proof," she retorted.

"Whatever proof you think you have is inaccurate; those games are only T," Cath replied, while a little crowd gathered around them.

"I looked it up on the Internet myself, and the new *Navy SEALs* game is M. There is article after article telling how horribly it influences the emerging mind. But what should we expect from a mother who lets her daughter date before she's sixteen?"

Cath felt like she had been slapped in the face. Sandra had been with *her* son, and if Hillary had so much as informed her, it never would have gotten this far. Cath closed her mouth quickly before she could say something she might regret. She stood silently, feeling surrounded by people who had shown her no affection and now were giving her no support, and looked at Hillary hopelessly.

"I am done discussing this with you. If you have any other points to discuss, please send it to me in letter form by Wednesday."

Hillary opened her mouth, ready for a retort, but Cath put the flat of her palm in front of her face and turned to walk away, determined not to say another word.

"You can't do this. My perspective has validity," Hillary almost screamed.

Cath ignored her entirely and marched to her van. She jumped in and closed the door, trying to hold back the tears. Sandra climbed into the passenger seat a few minutes later and put her hand over her mother's. "Wow, Mom, she's madder at you than I am."

Within minutes her boys must have heard about the altercation because they silently slunk into the backseat and Cath turned the ignition. At least Sandra was talking to her again.

❋ duct tape can't fix everything

The first day of school was always a letdown for Cath. She dropped off the children and went back home to a mostly empty house and immediately missed them all. She and Mike did the dishes together and went for a walk to the real pond down the street to feed the ducks. After lunch he took a nap and she read the next few chapters of Sherry Dew's latest book. Finally, she pulled out some cookie sheets, covered them with wax paper, and made no-bake cookies out of oatmeal, cocoa, and peanut butter. Her children loved them and called them Dog Poop Cookies because of their resemblance to the real thing. Mike woke up at the smell of the confection, and they both licked the pan.

The children exploded through the door at three thirty, excited about their new adventures. They spoke of their teachers, potential friends, and after-school activities they wanted to join—all except Carson. He sat in the corner molding his cookie into some strange shape and not saying a word. After the others had run off to go finish homework or shoot some hoops, Cath walked around the island and sat next to her ten-year-old boy, a difficult age for any kid. Putting an arm around him, he turned to his mother and began to tear up. "Mom, you might as well know that you're going to get a phone call from Mr. Ryder."

"Why?" Cath asked openly.

"Well, to get to know us better he asked all the kids what they would invent if they could make anything. It was stupid. All the other kids were saying cars and motorcycles that are already invented. It was driving me crazy. So when it got to my turn, I said a bomb with an infrared censor that could detect when all living matter was off the property. Then it would explode, destroying the school without hurting anybody. I only said it because I wanted them all to stop. Some of the girls screamed that I was a terrorist, and the teacher got really mad and made me stay in at recess. Now, I'd like to know, what is wrong with what I said? It wouldn't hurt anybody, and school is stupid."

Cath hugged her struggling pre-teen and said, "When I was a kid, your teacher would have laughed at that and given you an A for ingenuity. But in today's world, there are people so unhappy and desperate, they would really do something like that. Carson, you've got to grow up a little too fast. I'm sorry, but it is just the reality of the world we live in. So no more talk about bombing the school, and I'll smooth things over with your new teacher. Deal?"

"You mean, you're not mad at me?" He smiled.

"I think you're funny and brilliant. Want another cookie?"

Carson popped the one in front of him in his mouth. "Sure."

The next morning was Mike's first day at preschool. Cath decided to go walking around the lake later—the lake where she had gone jogging with Tandy. She hoped with enough effort she could get to the point where she could jog all the way around. At ten she dropped Mike off. She looked for Pattie but didn't see her anywhere. There were no women in the hall either, so Cath supposed the matter had finally been settled. She was surprised that there were so many children in the basement and that most of the helpers were very young, unlike the older grandmas she had seen earlier.

When Cath got to the lake, it was crowded with young mothers pushing strollers and groups of women walking and talking in friendly conversation. As she started around the path, she found herself listening in on a group of neighbors walking in front of her who obviously had known each other for years. They were laughing about their husbands' funny antics and asking about each other's grown children. Cath wondered if she would ever be able to have a circle of friends like that, but then she stopped herself. There was no value in this sort of thinking, Cath thought angrily. She knew if she listened to much more, she would just make herself more depressed, so she passed the group at a jog and kept going. All the stupid remarks that Lynnette and Hillary slung at her on Sunday filled her mind and pushed her forward faster. It felt good driving herself to the limit of her capacity, getting away from it all, and leaving the other walkers in the dust. As she rounded the corner, Cath suddenly realized how badly her lungs were burning and her side was aching. She stopped and dropped her hands to her knees, trying to catch her breath.

As she did, Tandy ran up behind her and stopped. "Wow, Cath, you've been practicing."

Cath waved at Tandy, unable to say anything, gulping in the air in huge gasps.

"I just wanted you to know that we are very impressed with the way you handled Hillary. With the Relief Society president on vacation, she has taken over everything, and we're sick of it. It was nice to see someone put her in her place. Well, ta-ta."

Tandy lit off at an effortless pace, and Cath shook her head and walked slowly the rest of the way, feeling awful that her behavior would encourage that sort of unkindness. Half an hour later she limped into the Pleasant Valley Home for the Elderly and went up to the front desk. Sonja was sitting there looking bored. It was that funny time of the morning, before lunch and after morning rounds, when there was a lull in activity. She looked up and seemed happy to see a familiar face. "Hi, Mrs. Reed. Do you have a second?" the nurse asked timidly.

"Call me Cath." She nodded and leaned her elbows against the counter.

Sonja looked down at the paper she had in her hands and kept flicking the corner nervously. "How did you like your letter from Gwen?"

"The truth?" Cath scrunched up her nose. "Well, it wasn't just a letter; it was like a homework assignment. I'm here to report on it, but I don't think my answer is going to be good enough," Cath said, relieved to have someone to share her feelings with.

"Me too . . . only I haven't done mine yet, and I've been scared to death that she'd wake up and I'd have to face her empty-handed. You know, I deal with little old ladies all day and can usually just shake off what they tell me, but she's different. I feel like if I don't do it, I'll let her down or something. And for some reason, I don't want to do that."

"So what is your challenge?" Cath peeked over the edge of the counter at the letter Sonja held.

"You first," Sonja said seriously.

"Fine. Mine was to do something fun. I thought my whole life was fun, but when it came to intentionally doing something fun, just for me—well, I've really had a hard time, believe it or not."

Sonja laughed. "Just looking at you, I believe it. You wouldn't know a good time if it jumped up and hit you in the face."

"Ow," Cath said, feigning injury. "Now yours. What does Gwen want you to do?" She smiled, feeling surprisingly comfortable with the banter between them.

Sonja became silent. She took a shuddering breath and looked up. "She wants me to talk to you about the Church. She said that I could ask you anything—any question at all. Then she wants me to tell her what I asked and what I thought about it. That's all." Sonja bowed her head, and Cath knew from the little she had been told that so many powerful emotions were tangled up in what Sonja understood of the truth that just going there hurt her deeply.

"You are so brave," Cath said without thinking.

"Brave?"

"Sonja, facing a situation where you have been hurt and trying to figure it all out is really scary and painful. The fact that you are considering it is . . . brave. I think you are wonderful."

Sonja smiled. "Well, when do you want to get together?" she asked. "I was thinking about lunch on Thursday?"

"I already have a visiting teaching appointment on Thursday. I finally got in touch with that last name on my list, and I still have a preschooler home, but next week at this time would be great. He'd be in school. What do you say?"

Sonja nodded and buzzed her in. "She better not wake up before then or I'll tell her it was your fault, Cath," she said, trying out her name for the first time. Cath smiled and headed on back to write her report to Gwen about the hidden treasure, wondering if Gwen remembered the organ.

The next day Cath attacked the laundry room with Mike at her side; she had a goal to do one fun thing while each load was washing. First, she took her preschooler out to the railroad tracks and tried to flatten a penny. The older boys had done it a couple of times, but Cath was amazed at how fun it was. She saved two for Gwen. Then she got strawberry buckets and made a cricket cage while her son tried to catch a creature to put in it. Mike found a fat toad camouflaged in the gravel beside the driveway, but the poor creature looked so miserable in their little prison that they let it go after a few minutes.

Finally, they got out the butcher paper and outlined Mike's body, then turned him into a life-size superhero. He decided to be Toad Man, who could leap tall buildings in a single bound. The emblem on his chest resembled the little friend that they had freed earlier. After lunch, Mike napped as Cath put away the clothes, when she suddenly remembered she had promised Carson she would talk to his teacher. She picked up the phone and dialed the school's number, hoping she could catch him during lunch. She was put right through and set an appointment. As she hung up, the phone rang again. Cath jumped at the sound. She couldn't remember the last person who'd called her. She lifted the receiver hopefully and answered.

"Sister Reed, I'm Sister Gunnell, the Primary president. I think we've met. Anyway, we're looking for someone to cover Cub Scouts today. I know it's short notice, but Jenny's sick and Barb is expecting a baby and is on bed rest for the next few weeks, so we are really in a bind."

As Cath listened to her rattle off the names, she could feel the closeness of these women, serving side by side, and wanted so badly to have a calling, to feel a part of something. It had been almost two months, and she still felt brand new to the area.

Cath responded emphatically, "I'd love to. What have they been working on?"

"I have no idea. I've never had a child in the program, so I just let Jenny do what she wants."

"That's fine," Cath chimed in. "I'll come up with something." As she set down the receiver, Carson and Jordan burst through the door, and Cath told them that they could have apples and peanut butter for their after-school snack. Carson ran into the kitchen, but Jordan stopped to show his mother his new acquisition.

"Mom, look at this. There is this group of guys in shop class, and the teacher lets all of us eat lunch in his room. They always do something fun in there and today we made these."

He handed her a silver plastic wallet, complete with little compartments for credit cards. He had three dollars in the billfold.

"Wow, this is very cool." Cath smiled.

Jordan grinned back. "It's made completely out of duct tape."

"Really?" Cath said, doing a double take. "Now that you say it, I can see but I never would have guessed. Would you mind showing me how to do this? I need something for Scouts. They asked me to substitute."

Three hours later, Cath was headed to the church with eight pieces of cardstock and six rolls of duct tape. She didn't want to upset Kevin, so she left his last roll in the work bench. Why anyone needed that much duct tape, she'd never know. As her van pulled into the parking lot, Winlyn ran up with a group of friends asking if she was doing Cubs. None of them had on uniforms, and it was a challenge for the boys to keep their arms folded during the prayer, but Cath complimented the boys who at least made an effort and then pulled out Jordan's shop wallet. It was being passed around the room when Bishop Miller stuck in his head. "What are you guys up to?" he asked.

The boys hopped up and ran to the door excitedly, showing off the wallet they were going to make. Bishop Miller took it in his hands and looked at it closely. Cath could see a sparkle in his eye. She said, "You're welcome to join us. We have plenty of materials."

It didn't take much to bend his arm, and within a few minutes, long sticky bands of duct tape were being unwound and ripped from their rolls. Two of the most precocious boys slapped theirs together, and the finished product looked like a wad of used tape. Winlyn was trying harder, but his wallet was looking almost as wrinkled as Sister Witherby, the old organist. Carson and another little boy named Kyle sat beside Bishop Miller, slowly assembling each piece of their wallets with precision and smoothing out every air bubble. In the middle of the activity, Sister Jacobs stuck her head in the room. She opened her mouth to say something and then saw Bishop Miller.

"I need to speak with you after," she ordered and slammed the door.

Cath had almost forgotten about Sunday. She wondered if she should stick to her guns and only accept a letter or if she should just avoid the entire situation altogether. She turned and tried to focus on the boys.

When the last three were finished, Cath was very impressed.

They were better than the original. Bishop Miller looked proud of himself, took out his old beaten leather wallet, and began putting his credit cards and license into the new one. He got to the billfold and handed Kyle and Carson each a dollar bill. "Don't forget to pay your tithing." He smiled at them, and after the prayer the two boys ran out the door to show off their booty. Grinning, Bishop Miller came up to Cath and shook her hand. "Thanks, I needed to just have fun. We all have to do that sometime, you know?" Cath nodded, thinking of Gwen, and he left.

As she began to pick up the scraps of paper and scrunched up tape from the floor, Hillary arrived. She closed the door meaningfully without saying a word and stared at Cath for a full minute like she was a naughty child.

"What?" Cath finally asked.

"Sister Reed, I am so disappointed in you."

It had been a good day, and Cath decided that anything she said would be wrong. So, picking up her things, she opened the door and stepped into the hall.

"Sister Jacobs, I've really got to be going." Cath began walking away, but Hillary Jacobs would not allow it and ran around to head her off.

"No, Sister Reed, this is about something over which I have authority and something you totally ignored." Hillary looked right and left and began to whisper loudly, trying not to cause a scene, but a crowd of youth were already gathering. "Your visiting teaching assignment—you were supposed to only send letters. You had no right contacting those people. Lynnette told me how you injured her child and have been bothering the staff at the nursing home. If you can't learn to obey the rules, we may just have to release you."

Cath looked at the woman before her and shook her head. "Can I ask you something? Am I allowed to talk to my neighbors? Am I allowed to call friends and chat with them? Am I allowed to make new friends and visit or have lunch? Or even have them barge into my house uninvited?"

"Well, of course," Hillary stammered.

"That is all I did, and if you want to know, as of tomorrow, I will have 100 percent real visiting teaching. Talking, relating, teaching, learning, and touching visiting teaching. Not just sending a copied page from the *Ensign*. If the Relief Society president wants to make changes when she comes back, please have her contact me, Madam Secretary, but until then get out of my way!"

Cath grabbed her bags and marched to the door. She could hear a few of the teenagers in the hall clapping at the display. She peeked over her shoulder and saw Sandra standing next to Zee.

"Way to go, Sister R," he said to her with a thumbs up.

Sandra smiled. "Go, Mom."

Practically running to the car, Cath slammed the door and sunk into the driver's seat in total humiliation. She knew she had gone too far. She should have followed her instincts and just left. Cath knew her behavior was shameful. Sandra came rushing out to the car, followed by Carson and Jordan.

"Mom, you were awesome." Sandra beamed enthusiastically. "Zee says you are his hero. He has never seen anyone take his mom down like that. After you left, she totally broke down."

"Oh, should I go back now and apologize?" Cath began stepping out.

Jordan grabbed the door. "Mom, I saw her leaving and I think you better let her cool down a little. What did you say to her?"

"I'm not sure."

"I know," said Carson. "It's the same thing you say to me when I want to sleep in for church or don't clean my room—Mom guilt."

Cath told the children to get in the car and drove away slowly. She kept praying as she drove that she would somehow be able to fix this.

✱ he that hath ears to hear

When Cath drove up her driveway, she saw that Kevin had unexpectedly arrived home from his business trip early. The children hopped out and exploded through the front door, surrounding their father, each telling their version of what had happened. Cath slowly grabbed her things out of the car and stepped into the room with her head down. Kevin walked forward and gave her a hug. "Sounds like it was a tough night."

"That's pretty accurate." She buried her head in her husband's shoulder and finally allowed herself a good cry. The children took the cue from their father's stern glances and went upstairs while he led his wife to the sofa and sat down.

"I tried to just walk away, but she followed me so that the conversation was in the hall—in front of everyone. I don't think Hillary Jacobs will ever forgive me for this." Cath pulled away from Kevin and put her head in her hands.

"It may not be as bad as you think, Cath; things like this happen all the time at work. Emotions run high and sometimes people just lose it."

"So how do you fix it? How do you make it better?" Cath implored.

Kevin stretched his arms up in the air and folded his hands

confidently behind his head. "You don't. It was a mistake. If you have apologized and promise to never do it again, the key is to move on. All you have to do is pretend it never happened. The next time you see her, don't avoid her but go straight up and shake her hand. Compliment her on something nice and walk away. Eventually it will fade away and be completely forgotten."

Cath turned to her husband and rolled her eyes. "But what if she brings it up, or anyone else for that matter—I mean, the whole ward was there."

Kevin smiled and shook his head. "Doesn't matter. You just change the subject, compliment the person, and move on. It really works. Try it."

She nodded slightly. "I will."

The next morning Cath got the kids off to school and packed Mike in the car. When she turned the corner to his preschool, it was like a traffic jam. She had noticed more children every time she came, but this was ridiculous. She parked a block away and went to walk Mike in but was stopped by a girl in her early twenties with numerous tattoos and torn jeans who stood at the door. "Parents are not allowed." She put her hand up and took Mike, lining him up unceremoniously with a number of other children in the hall. "Pick up time for half days is eleven thirty." Cath left feeling disappointed again that she hadn't seen Pattie.

Twenty minutes later Cath turned left on the little cobblestone street beside the library, found number 402, and pulled to a stop. The cheery white Cape Cod with green shutters sparkled with its overflowing flowerbeds and lush green lawn. Then she realized that the numbers corresponded with the driveway and not the house that they were nearest. Four-o-two was really a small, dark-shingled bungalow with a very steep roofline. The yard was mostly weeds, and one pink shutter hung half off its hinges, paled by the sun. Taking a deep breath, she tightened her grip around her *Ensign* and marched forward to ring the doorbell. With this house, Cath knew she would get 100 percent visiting teaching this month.

She waited a few minutes and was starting to worry that Alexia wasn't home when suddenly the door flew open and there stood a middle-aged woman in an old house coat with her phone still in hand. "Cath, I'm so happy you're here. Come in, come in. I'll be right with you." She went back to her conversation, while Cath walked into the dark living room and sat down. "Lynnette, she's here. I've got to go. I'll call you later and tell you every detail, promise."

She hung up and smiled at Cath the way a cat smiles at its prey. But Cath sat up straight and vowed that she would not let it bother her in the least. "I'm Cath Reed, and I don't believe we have met."

"Oh, I know who you are. You have created quite a splash in the ward. I'm tempted to actually go on Sunday, just to see what you will do next." She raised her eyebrows and giggled wickedly, exposing her coffee-stained teeth.

Cath looked down at the pages she was holding, feeling uncomfortable. "It would be wonderful if you came on Sunday, I hope to see you there."

Alexia raised her eyebrows and giggled wickedly, exposing her coffee-stained teeth. "Oh, and you even brought a lesson for me? This is rich. Well, go on. I want to hear it."

Cath looked down at the pages she was holding, feeling very uncomfortable. She wished she had a real companion, but remembering her husband's words that morning about being pleasant and moving on, she swallowed deeply and began, "This month's lesson is on eternal marriage. We know that the greatest opportunity for happiness is within the bonds of an eternal marriage, and those who do not have that gift in this life will be given it later, if they are worthy."

"No thanks," said Alexia with a swish of her hand. "I can

handle men in small doses, but for eternity? Forget it." She laughed harshly and Cath put down the magazine.

"Alexia, do you have any children?"

"My son is twenty-two or something, and he's just as bad as the rest of them. I can't stand being around him for more than a couple of hours," she said, laughing. Knowing that it would be useless to continue with the lesson, Cath wanted to understand where Alexia was coming from, "So, Alexia, why did you join the Church? Tell me about your conversion."

Alexia stopped laughing and thought about it for a second. "You know, it was about twelve years ago that the missionaries taught me. They were really clever boys, and at first I thought the Church had a lot of answers. But as soon as the honeymoon stage was over, I saw what a total mess everything was. Lessons weren't prepared, the talks were so boring, and I grew out of it. Do you know that Bishop Miller doesn't even have a high school diploma and works a minimum-wage job? Once someone with half a brain becomes the leader there, maybe I'll come back."

Cath couldn't believe her ears. "Joseph Smith didn't have a high school diploma."

Alexia laughed. "That shows how little you know. Hillary told me that in Joseph's day his parents were landowners, which were actually the upper middle class. Bishop Miller works as a machinist at a newspaper printer. He has been doing the same low paying job for the last twenty-five years. How smart is that?"

"I've found him to be a kind and inspired bishop," Cath said sincerely, but Alexia just rolled her eyes. Looking around the room with every curtain drawn, dark-brown paneling and carpets, trash heaped in the corners, and a single light barely illuminating the center of the room, Cath felt sorry for this lonely woman living in the dark but wondered what else she could do.

"If you need anything please call me. I'd like to leave with a prayer," she said and left with a simple blessing that her eyes would be open to see the truth when they were ready. Walking outside, Cath took in the fresh air.

As she began walking to her car, a small red Focus pulled up in front of the cute little house next door. Pattie threw open her door and hopped out, carrying two bags of groceries. She left the door open, and Cath could see she had a few more inside. She hurried up to her. "Hey, Pattie, do you remember me?"

She smiled weakly. "Oh, Mrs. Reed. What are you doing here?"

"I was visiting your neighbor. She's a member of our church."

"Does she go more often than when she was a member of ours?" She raised her eyebrows.

"Nope," Cath said relaxing. "Let me help you." She ran to Pattie's car and grabbed the last two bags of groceries, and they headed to the door together. As Pattie threw it open, Cath gasped. It was incredible. Every wall was painted a different bright color with a silhouette of a child stenciled in the same hue but a darker tone. On the left, a child was discovering a flower. On the front wall, a girl was chasing a butterfly. In the dining room, a child was reading a book. In contrast, the entryway was a collage of different rectangles of every color around the house with little white frames of happy children dotting the wall symmetrically. There must have been over five hundred of them. They covered both the walls and the ceiling of the small entry. Each portrait was a work of art, exposing something unique and beautiful about that child. Cath paused and gaped at the glory of it. Turning to Pattie she smiled. "This is exquisite."

Pattie laughed modestly. "You are too kind. This is not good for my ego." She walked into the kitchen and Cath followed awkwardly. As she started to put away groceries, Pattie said wistfully, "They are all my kids from school. I remember all their names and love every one of them."

"I've missed you the last couple of days at preschool." Cath was surprised she had said it.

Pattie turned her back to Cath and started taking short breaths, trying to keep her emotions in check.

"What is it?" Cath asked, concerned.

"I quit the school. The women in the hall hired a lawyer and said they would shut us down if we didn't accept them."

"They couldn't have done that. It's not legal, is it?" Cath retorted.

"No, but it gave the senate of our church just enough of a nudge to roll over. Two days ago our pastor called me in and wanted to talk to me." Pattie looked at her friend for a while and then sighed. "Why don't you sit down; it's a long story." They walked into the front room, with its gleaming wood floors and soft sheepskin rugs. Her furniture was white and contemporary with big colorful pillows that mirrored the happy colors of the walls. Palms and ferns in generous white clay pots softened the corners of the room.

"What bothers me most," continued Pattie emphatically, "is that the things I've always known to be true, that I just assumed my church believed also, seem to be my own wishful thinking. I'm having such a hard time swallowing that."

"Like what?" Cath asked sincerely interested.

"The pastor sat me down and said that all my concerns about supporting mothers and encouraging families to remain intact were secondary to our primary goal. He told me that those are only temporary relationships anyway and that in heaven we are all just brothers and sisters with no parents and no children. The important thing is that they are raised to believe in Christ, and it doesn't really matter who does it." Pattie shook her head. "I can't believe that. It doesn't feel right, you know?"

Cath looked down at the *Ensign* in her hand, still turned to the page on forever families and celestial marriage. Her fingers burned, but she didn't want to stress out this friendship so early. There would be time later to share her beliefs, she thought. She didn't want to seem fanatical, so Cath simply nodded and let her friend go on.

"I have always thought that the reason God chose the title Father and Son was because family is the most important thing of all. I had hoped that when I married—if I ever get married—it would be forever. Do you believe your marriage is forever? That you will still be the mother of your children after you are in heaven?"

Okay! Cath almost shouted to the heavens. Taking a deep breath, she looked in Pattie's moistened eyes. "You are not going to believe this. I mean, I know this must sound like I planned it, but I was over at Alexia's house sharing a message from the Church. It comes out every month. Well, you wouldn't believe it if I told you, so just read it for yourself. Here."

Unsure of what she was talking about, Pattie took the *Ensign* and looked at the title of the visiting teaching message, reading it out loud: "A Forever Family: The Gift of an Eternal Marriage. We know that the greatest opportunity for happiness is within the bonds of an eternal marriage and those who do not have that gift in this life will be given it later, if they are worthy." Pattie put her hand to her lips and began to cry, reading silently to herself. The Spirit filled the room and Cath watched her eyes light up with truth. She sat quietly and let the Spirit be the teacher. When she had finished the article, she turned to Cath in disbelief. "This is what Mormons really believe?" Cath nodded. "We were taught that you were a cult and worshipped some crackpot named Joe Smith," Pattie said innocently.

"I imagine the same thing was said about the early Christians," Cath quipped.

"Touché." Pattie smiled.

"We actually worship Christ but believe that a lot of the truths he taught were lost during the dark ages. Great reformers like Luther and Moore opened the door for the truth to be fully restored through a modern prophet, just like prophets of old."

Pattie brought her attention back to the *Ensign* and turned the page. "Wow, I am so ready for this, but I want to make sure

I'm not leaping at something just to make myself feel better. I have had my whole life turned upside down, and I have to take baby steps. Can you understand that?"

Cath nodded, watching her friend still poring over the words. After a few minutes Pattie continued, "Can I keep this?"

"Sure," Cath said standing up. "Pattie, if you need anything feel free to call me. Here's my number." She reached in her bag and pulled out a slip of paper and wrote her number on the back. As she walked back to her car, Cath thought about the two houses side by side that had been given the same message and how differently it had been received.

❋ surprises—pleasant and not

When Cath got home, something was not right. She could feel it. Mike was exhausted after preschool so she gave him a snack, put him down for a nap, and then walked through each room, looking for clues. As she stepped into the kitchen, she caught sight of the large calendar on the wall and gasped. So that was why Kevin had planned on cutting his business trip short.

Grabbing her purse, she suddenly noticed the blinking light on the phone and pushed the button to listen to the message. "Mom, it's Sandra. I'm staying after school to join Computer Club. I just heard about it. I should be really late because it's the first meeting. I'll phone if I need a ride home. Love you."

Cath shook her head slowly, feeling confused; Sandra had never really shown an interest in computers. Just then Carson and Jordan burst through the door, threw their backpacks down on the counter, and turned to run up to the bonus room when Cath called out, "Boys, I've got a problem and really need your help, but it's a secret." The word *secret* stopped them in their tracks, and they rushed back and listened as their mother whispered how she wanted each of them to prepare for the surprise. Then she hurried out the door.

There was only forty-five minutes before Kevin would arrive home when Cath lugged in the last of the groceries. Everyone was rushing around in excitement with poster paints, tape, candles, and fine china being thrown around the kitchen and out the back door. Mike had been acting as lookout and ran in, informing the crew he had seen Dad's car. The final touches were put in place and everything else was unceremoniously stuffed in the closet. He entered the door and immediately smiled at the large sign that read "Happy Anniversary!"

Kevin acted surprised, and Carson put a blindfold on his father and led him out the back door to the four-star restaurant they had created on the back deck. A card table and two chairs were set up with a single lit candle in the center. The table was covered with a peach plastic tablecloth and green placemats, their wedding colors. Two place settings of the best china were laid out, complete with salad and dessert forks, and the napkins were folded like turkeys sitting on the plates, a Thanksgiving family tradition that had expanded to envelop every formal occasion. Kevin grinned and pulled out his wife's chair while the children ran back in the house. They emerged a few minutes later dressed as waiters, and each brought out a delicious dish to the table, thanks to Hy-Vee's eight-person Chinese dinner special. Then Jordan and Carson serenaded them with a recorder and trumpet duet of "Ode to Joy." Kevin looked at his wife and handed her a small package. She lifted the lid. It was a necklace with a little silver dove charm on it. Cath held it in the light of the full moon and smiled. "So what is this for?"

"Cath, I know this has been a hard move for you and that I haven't been here as much as either of us would like, but when I saw this dove, I thought of you. You are so close to the Spirit and I know you listen to its promptings. I just hoped that if you wore this, it would help comfort you a little."

Cath smiled. It was a beautiful piece of jewelry and a sweet sentiment. Kevin stepped over and fastened the delicate chain around her neck, and Cath turned and put her arms around her husband when suddenly Mike came running outside shouting, "The police are here! Hurry!" The flashing lights shone through the kitchen windows, and the whole family rushed out front to a waiting squad car.

A uniformed officer stood on the front porch, and Cath ran up to him frantically and Kevin stepped up behind her. "Is this the residence of Sandra Reed?" the officer asked.

Cath covered her mouth and tears formed in her eyes. "Has something happened to her?"

Seeing the concern in their eyes, he quickly shook his head. "She's fine. We just had a minor disturbance. It seems that she stayed after school with a Zeniff Jacobs and the two decided to go visit a friend. Unfortunately that friend was on vacation, and a neighbor saw them breaking in. We don't know yet if the owners want to press charges."

With nothing more to say, the policeman opened the back door and Sandra walked up to her parents with her head bowed. Cath was filled with conflicting emotions, but as the officer began to leave she ran up to thank him. He was a small man, and she had the feeling she had met him before but shook it off.

Kevin had taken the family inside and Cath followed. Father and daughter were already talking in Sandra's room when Cath arrived. "Dad, the school was closing and we didn't have any place to go. Zee said he had permission. We didn't hurt anything, just sat in the front room and talked. It's no big deal."

"Well, I happen to think that whenever you get brought home by a police officer that it is a big deal—a very big deal. You are grounded—two weeks. When school is not in session, you will be in the presence of your mother or me. End of story."

"But, Dad!" Sandra looked from parent to parent and flopped on her bed in defeat. After Cath and Kevin left the room, she turned to him. "I thought the Zee thing was over—I had no idea this was going on. That is exactly the right answer. Thank you."

Kevin looked embarrassed. "With my traveling, I've really just sentenced *you* to a two-week grounding. Sorry."

Cath laughed. "That's my job."

✻ facing problems head-on

Cath was not looking forward to going to church. She had chosen not to call the Jacobs about the incident since she couldn't think of anything to say. All Cath wanted from the day was to not have another confrontation. At least with Kevin in town Cath had hope. They arrived fifteen minutes before the meeting started and sat in the third row. Cath sat next to Sandra, listening to the prelude music and silently wondering when she could get another chance to play the organ. She looked at her daughter, tempted to tell her about the secret treasure, when suddenly Carson jumped up and ran up the aisle. Cath turned and saw the bishop with his wife at his side. Jordan was sitting on the front row, waiting to pass the sacrament, and his face lit up when he saw them. Cath slid past her daughter and walked over to them. "Jerri, how great to see you. It's been too long."

"You bet it has," Carson interjected. "Are you coming over tomorrow to play?"

Jerri shook her head, "Sorry, trooper, but I've got to go out of town for business. I get back next week."

"What about next Saturday night?" Cath suggested. "We could have a barbecue."

"Sounds great. And you better practice, Carson." Jerri smiled and the bishop walked up to the stand and took his seat. Jordan and Sandra had joined the conversation. "You're sitting with us, right?"

It was decided, and they all sat down just as the meeting was beginning. With Jerri beside them, Hillary didn't dare approach, and surprisingly very few others did either. As they left the building, Cath wondered how many of the people around her felt as unwelcome as she did. Maybe they just didn't know how to reach out of their shells. Again she wished that she would be given a calling—it just made it so much easier to get to know people.

The next Tuesday, after dropping Mike off at preschool, Cath drove to the old downtown area. Sonja had agreed to meet her at The Blue Heron, a little coffeehouse in an old factory building. The walls were rustic brick, the big front window was made of poured glass, and distressed wooden booths edged the room. The ceiling was two stories high, and every wall was covered with old street signs, rusty bicycles, baseball paraphernalia, and framed posters of Pleasant Valley over the last century. The counter was at the very back of the store with a large sign above it, detailing your choices, which primarily focused on many varieties of coffee products. Cath asked for hot chocolate and a cranberry muffin. With her selections in hand, she chose a booth to the side of the room and waited, a little worried that Sonja might stand her up.

Picking up the *USA Today*, Cath began reading and was soon lost in meaningless special interest stories. Some time had passed when she heard a sigh and looked up. Sonja had a huge mug of steaming coffee in her hand and tentatively sat down across from her. The poor woman looked exhausted, and Cath put down the paper, knowing that this meeting had been a great source of stress for her. "Sonja, it's so good to see you."

"You were worried I wasn't going to show, weren't you?" Sonja wouldn't meet Cath's gaze.

"The thought had crossed my mind," Cath admitted.

"Well, I almost didn't." She sipped her coffee and then drummed her fingers against the sides of the large mug nervously. "I've been up all night trying to figure out what I wanted to ask. I'd come up with something and then I'd think, 'That's not the point.' It was like digging through layers and layers of crap."

Cath shook her head and wished she could do something to help her but knew all she could do was listen.

"This whole thing seemed a waste of time and I was just going to blow it off, when it hit me. There is something that I really want to know. So here it is . . . When I was eighteen my father died and my mother had a nervous breakdown."

Cath covered her mouth. "I am so sorry."

"Well, believe it or not, that isn't the worst of it." She took another sip of coffee, trying to contain her emotions, and continued, "My uncle who lived in the next town was supposed to be a righteous Mormon. He was even part of that High Great Council thingy. Anyway, he would have nothing to do with us—said we were too much trouble. So I took care of my sister. It was going okay until the stupid Relief Society president stuck her nose into it. She called social services and had my sister thrown into foster care. I never saw her again."

"Oh, Sonja, how awful for you." Cath reached her hand across the table.

"It's past history." The toughness was back in her voice. Sonja lifted her chin and looked straight at Cath. "So here is my question. This is what I need to know. If my uncle was a true Mormon, then why wouldn't he take us in?" She began to tear up but spoke emphatically through the tears. "Why wouldn't he love us?"

Cath stared at this brokenhearted child. Her body may have been grown, but her heart was that of a neglected teenager. She wanted to throw her arms around her and comfort her. "Sonja, I don't know why your uncle made the choices he did, but I do know that if I had been there, I would have taken care of you and your family. I would have let you come live with us and would have done whatever it took to help you as you grieved for that great loss. I would have loved you. I am so sorry." She reached out and gently touched her hand.

Sonja closed her eyes and the tears flowed for a long time. Cath waited until she was ready to say something. "I believe you, but isn't the Church supposed to make people better? Don't they have rules about this sort of thing? How could they just let that happen? I mean, you should have seen this Relief Society president. She was just a witch, and my uncle was almost as bad. I could have taken care of my younger brother and sister—we had enough money. All I wanted was a little help, but they didn't want any part of it—of us. They pretended to be so much better than us because they went to church, but they were really just total selfish jerks." She was getting worked up about it and sipped her coffee again.

"I believe you," Cath said, reflecting on the recent experiences in her new ward, "and I'll warn you that if you did come back to church here, you may meet other jerks that claim to be part of the Lord's Church. But I think sometimes our concept of what it means to be a member is not necessarily accurate."

"What do you mean?" Sonja asked.

"Don't think I'm crazy, but I believe being a member is more like . . ." she thought for a minute and her mind drifted back to Ralph Beckman, "playing the organ."

"You are whack!" Sonja shook her head and laughed.

"Hear me out. Lately, I've learned something really interesting about the organ at our church. It's called a Barton organ and is one of very few. The pipes are said to be silver-voiced, and according to an article I read, one Barton organ actually shattered all the windows and lights of an entire stadium when played with all the stops pulled."

"Awesome." Sonja rested her chin in her cupped hand and listened.

Cath continued, "Other organs may look more impressive, but the music created by a Barton can be the most beautiful in the world, depending on who's playing it. Right now our organist is a sweet woman who has very little ability. Most of the notes are wrong, and from hearing her play, you'd never guess the potential of the instrument she's using."

"I get it. So it's just that they are rotten organists. And that's supposed to make me feel better?" Sonja rolled her eyes.

"Look at it more closely, Sonja. You could spend your whole life analyzing why others don't play well. Perhaps they were never taught how to play properly or refused to practice or are like the naughty little boys who slam on the keys after church. Whatever the reasons that they made mistakes doesn't really matter when it comes to your choices. Now let's look at you. Because of them, you've chosen to not even try and to walk away from the most beautiful and glorious experiences of your life."

"I did, didn't I?" Sonja nodded, still contemplating the idea.

"What is so unfortunate is to think about how you, Sonja, could be so incredible with this gift, but you'll never know until you try—until you come back and throw yourself into it." Cath continued, "I know it's hard when you have been so hurt, but the thing I have to constantly remind myself is that there is a huge difference between the Church—which is true, perfect, and beautiful like the organ—and the organist, who are the people in it that might not be any of those things. The key is to not look to the right or to the left, but to look within your own heart and decide how you want to sound when it's your turn to play. Are you willing to fill yourself and others with all the light and beauty there is in store for you, and, if so, don't you think it is worth it to do the things that will bring you there?"

Putting her hand over her face, Sonja took a ragged breath and focused her attention on the surrounding walls. Cath sat quietly and waited for a few minutes, not sure of what Sonja thought about her words. Sonja finally turned. "I guess I could start by praying again."

"That would be a good start."

Shaking her head, Sonja whispered, "I've spent so many years being mad at God, I don't know if he'll even listen to me anymore."

"Oh, Sonja." Cath shook her head and smiled. "Your Heavenly Father loves you so much, and I bet he is as disappointed with the way you've been treated as you are, but he has given all of us the power to choose. That is why he will never force himself on you until you ask. He hasn't been part of your life because you chose for him not to be. But once you open the door, the very minute you invite him back in your life, you will feel his love wrap around you with both arms. I just know it."

Sonja nodded. "In some ways I already do." She pushed her mug to the side. "You know, I don't even like coffee. I just got it as a test to see if you would say anything."

"Well, I said a lot of things but nothing about the coffee. If you want me to nag you about it, I've got that down to an art form—just ask my kids." Both women laughed. An hour later, they left, feeling good about the morning. Sonja had a lot to think about and Cath wasn't going to rush her. Cath was smiling as she strolled past the little shops on her way to her car, when suddenly she caught sight of an antique clock in the window and started sprinting. She had totally forgotten about the appointment and was already fifteen minutes late.

By the time she entered the empty classroom, it was 12:32. Mr. Ryder had his books in hand and was preparing to leave. "Oh, we're late, are we? Like parent like child." His tone was condescending.

Cath walked forward quickly with her hand extended. "I'm so sorry. Do you still have time to meet with me or would you like to reschedule?" He ignored her hand and turned his back to her, slowly walking to the rear of the room and sitting at his desk, as if at a throne.

Watching him woke a frustration in Cath; she stood before him, refusing to sit down. "Mr. Ryder, I am very concerned. I know that the first day of school was difficult, but I have heard from my son that he has spent the last three recesses in this room without being able to give me a specific reason for the disciple. There seems to be a real communication gap here."

Mr. Ryder stood up. "Miss Reed, your son has been nothing but a problem in my class from the first day he has been here. He has forgotten his pencil on numerous occasions, and when I told him to bring two the next day to make up for it—do you know what he did?"

Cath shook her head, listening for some valid complaint. "He brought one," Mr. Ryder continued. "I sent him back to his locker to get another, and he took almost half an hour, missing his first test, which of course will permanently affect his grade. I will not have him disrupting my classroom. Is that understood?"

Carson had said that his teacher was a man who would not listen, but he had mentioned nothing about missing school supplies. The question now was whether or not this situation could be salvaged. Cath picked her words carefully. "Mr. Ryder, what can Carson or I do to improve his performance in your class?"

Mr. Ryder was in a tizzy and picked up his books, shaking his head nervously. "I don't know if there is anything he can do. I'm fighting years and years of poor habits, bad attitudes, and mythical indoctrination here, but what can I expect? With so many children, how can you ever keep them under control?"

Cath was sure he had heard about Sandra's ride home in a police car, but there was a phrase he had said that bothered her even more. "What do you mean by mythical indoctrination?"

Mr. Ryder began to talk slower, like he was addressing a small child. "I know you probably don't understand the effects of your culture and have very little education, but . . ."

"I have as much formal education as you do, Mr. Ryder. Now, what culture are you speaking of?" Cath responded emphatically.

Mr. Ryder continued without apology. "Didn't you move here from Utah? Theological legends aside, if you look at their educational statistics, they are among the lowest in the country. The largest single factor is family size, and you seem to be toeing the party line no matter what the consequences to our environment. Sometimes I wonder why Carson is even in my class. I am considering recommending that he be lowered a grade."

"Has Carson's homework been completed on time? Has he been disrespectful? Do you feel he is incapable of this level of work?" Cath asked, concerned.

"Not overtly, but his attitude is seriously lacking. In class discussions he refuses to accept established fact. It is quite common when students have been only exposed to one viewpoint their entire lives, but he refuses to see reason."

"Can you be more specific?" she asked, still unclear of the problem.

"Can I be totally frank? We have recently been covering certain social issues, and your son is blinded by indoctrination when it comes to population control, individual freedoms, and social reform. It is like his religious leanings not only put him on the fringe of society, but they have hampered his view of reality and it is horrifying to me."

"Wait a second," Cath looked at him, "are you saying that because he is Mormon and doesn't agree with your political standing, you think he should flunk?"

Mr. Ryder knew he had said too much and began back pedaling. "I said nothing of the kind, but I must admit it seriously bothers me that you claim to believe one thing and teach another. I have a friend who recently was exposed to some of your literature.

It was the most skewed drivel I've ever read. Do you even know what you really believe?"

As Cath looked at the disdain coming from the man before her, she stood tall. "Yes, Mr. Ryder, I believe that the true gospel of Christ has finally been restored in its fulness with a prophet to guide it. I believe that families are eternal and that there is a purpose to our lives here. I believe that if we listen to the Spirit, we will be guided in our decisions and find answers to our prayers, and I have not only reconciled those beliefs to current scripture, but I know of their truth through the Holy Ghost. So, Mr. Ryder, what do you believe?"

Mr. Ryder stared at the woman in front of him, speechless, and then said, "I believe that your son does not belong in my classroom."

"On that point, we are in total agreement. Carson does not belong in your class or in your presence. As of tomorrow, you will never speak to him again. He will either be switched to another classroom or be withdrawn from this school entirely, and, Mr. Ryder, I hope that from this point on you never let your personal opinions color how you treat a student again."

Cath rushed out the door and down the stairs to the crowded hallway—lunchtime was over and students were hurrying back to their classes. Her palms were sweaty and she was breathing hard. Never in her life had she seen such bitter disdain for the Church and any who belonged to it. Squeezing past bodies against the flow of traffic, Cath had almost made it to the back doors when the principal caught her. "Mrs. Reed, I believe we need to talk."

She turned, surprised, and wondered if he had already talked with Mr. Ryder and had a similar viewpoint. Cath had hoped to talk with her husband before approaching the principal and asked, "Are you sure this is a good time for you?"

The kind principal smiled and led her into his office, shutting the door. He invited her to sit down and then sat across from her. "I need to apologize. I heard you had an appointment with Carson's teacher today and guessed what it was concerning. Ken Ryder is a brilliant teacher, but he gets carried away sometimes." An hour later she emerged from his office with Carson's new schedule and an eased mind. Apparently, she wasn't the first disgruntled parent when it came to this teacher. When Cath asked how this was allowed to happen, the principal said that due to tenure, the administration's hands were tied. Cath suggested Mr. Ryder be made a lunch monitor, because although tenure insists he can't be fired, it does not specify his position. The principal laughed and happily switched Carson to the other class, begging her not to withdraw him. Cath left feeling confident that she had made the right decision.

✸ waterproof or regular mascara?

Sandra sat on the bathroom counter in her pajamas. "But, Mom, I have a big test on Monday. I promise I will work in my room the whole time."

Cath grabbed her lipstick and leaned toward the mirror. "No doing. Dad has to go to meet with the bishop, and being grounded means you are either with him or me. If you want to wait in the foyer at church for an hour, be my guest."

Sandra took the lipstick from her mother and put it on playfully. "All right, but we need to be back in an hour. Where is your shopping list?"

"In here." Cath pointed to her head with the mascara wand. Cath had paused for just a minute to decide whether to go with the regular mascara, which was easier to take off, or the waterproof. Since she couldn't see any cause for tears in the near future, regular won out.

"You know, Mother, if you had a shopping list, we could finish in half the time." Since Sandra had been grounded, she had become more and more demanding. Cath thought about her husband's comment about who was really being grounded and was beginning to agree. "I'll go get paper and pencil and meet you in the car in five minutes," Sandra ordered, dashing off.

Five minutes later the two drove down the road with Sandra trying desperately to extrapolate a shopping list from her mother. "What are we eating on Thursday for dinner?"

"I think we'll have chicken leftovers, so . . ." Cath said. Without really thinking, she put on the breaks and did a quick U-turn, heading for the Pleasant Valley Home for the Elderly.

Sandra was confused. "I thought we were going to the store."

"We were, but I just remembered it has been too long since I visited a friend. I will only be a second—I promise—I just know I have to do this. Why don't you finish the menu while I'm gone? You can choose whatever you want."

Surprisingly, Sandra didn't put up a fight, and Cath jumped out of the car and hurried to the front door. Sonja was at the desk and as soon as she saw Cath, she shook her head. "Not yet. Don't worry. The longest she has gone was six weeks. She still has another two to go before we start getting a little excited."

"Can I see her?" Cath asked, and Sonja buzzed her through. There was so much she had to share with her. She hadn't told her about Pattie's great experience or Sandra being grounded or the terrible discussion she had with Carson's teacher—now that would make a great picture. When she came to the door, another woman was sitting beside Gwen, holding her hand. Cath wasn't sure what to do and stood in the doorway awkwardly. The woman was bowing her head and sniffling, but the curly brown hair looked so familiar.

"Pattie?" Cath asked.

Pattie spun around, surprised, and quickly wiped her face with the back of her hand. "Cath? What are you doing here?"

"Gwen is a member of our church and I visit her monthly." The words sounded cold in her mouth—that didn't really explain it at all. How much she loved Gwen and needed her right now.

Pattie turned to Gwen and stared at her serene face. "Gwen was a Mormon? I mean, I knew she was religious, but she never said . . . or maybe I just never heard her and he almost had me convinced."

"What?" Cath asked confused.

"Sit down," Pattie said, pulling up the other chair. "It's only fair you know. When you left that magazine, the *Ensign*, at the house, I read every word. It was wonderful—like all the things I ever really thought were true were just laid out before me. I loved what it said about how families work and how to recognize the feeling of the Spirit whispering to your heart and how to feel forgiven. My favorite part was to think that God was a loving parent and Christ was my brother.

"Well, a few days after we talked, I shared the magazine with a close friend of mine who totally freaked out and said he would never speak to me again. The next day the pastor came by to try to convince me to go back to the center. It seems they've had some serious problems and are losing students. He saw the magazine on the table and almost had a fit, saying that I would lose my place in heaven and go to hell if I continued on that path. He told me that the things I had read were only what they taught certain members and that they kept secret what they really believed. He brought over some books that said some terrible things about the Mormons. I read them. When I asked why anyone would believe in this faith if these things were true, he said that the average Mormons didn't even know what they really believed and were dumb sheep."

"I've heard worse." Cath thought of Mr. Ryder and wondered if he was that friend.

"Well, I'm embarrassed to say that I believed them. I think that in some small way I wanted to, because it would be so much easier. I've gone to that church my whole life and can't imagine not being a part of it. But this morning when I went back to the childcare center, I knew I could never go back again. Do you know what they've done?"

Cath nodded. "It's pretty bad."

"The reason that the childcare center was so wonderful had very little to do with the facility. It was the women who loved being with children. Most of them had been wonderful mothers themselves who gave a few hours every day to play and share their genuine love because they knew they were giving value to the community. What we paid them was not a hundredth of what they were worth. Now all the experienced mothers have been fired and replaced with full-time minimum-wage employees who are little more than children themselves. This decision was based on the bottom line, not on the quality of care. That new director doesn't think about the children at all, and the church I used to go to has turned into nothing more than a business."

Suddenly there was a knock at the door, and they both looked over to see Sandra standing there. "Mom, are you almost done?" she asked.

"Who is this?" said Pattie, brightening up.

"This is Sandra, my fourteen-year-old."

Sandra was nervous, and when she got nervous, she talked. "We're on our way to the store to get stuff for a barbecue tonight. Sister Miller is bringing the games. She was a real marine, and the boys think it's going to be really fun, but she said that she would include me too. Is this woman in a coma?" Sandra looked down with sympathy at Gwen's peaceful face. "She looks sort of like a really old sleeping beauty."

Pattie stood up and put an arm around Sandra. "In a way she is. A long time ago, Gwen was my fourth grade teacher, believe it or not. It was the last year she taught. Gwen saved me. My parents were in the middle of a nasty divorce, but she was always there. She had this wonderful garden; it was like a fairyland, and she let me go there whenever things were getting crazy. It was so beautiful, you can hardly imagine it. You will need to come and visit me sometime and you can see her magical garden for yourself."

"You live there now?" Sandra asked.

"Yep," Pattie reminisced. "When Gwen started falling asleep and not waking up, she needed someone to help watch her. She never had children of her own, so I moved in with her. She is a wonderful person, as great as any character in a storybook."

Pattie bowed her head and Sandra blurted out, "Why don't you come to the barbecue tonight? It will be lots of fun."

"Oh, I couldn't," Pattie said, glancing in Cath's direction.

"We would love to have you, but I'll have to warn you, it may get kind of rowdy." She smiled.

Pattie thought for a while and then nodded. "I'll do it for Gwen. She'd want me to."

"That's great! I'll write out the directions for you," Cath said, grabbing a piece of paper off the nightstand and a brown crayon. After passing the note to Pattie, she turned back to the desk, "There is just one more thing I need to write to Gwen." She took another page and began to jot something down feverishly.

Pattie was staring at her and asked, "What are you writing? Was it you that started all this?"

Sandra piped up, "What? What did my mom do?"

Pattie turned to her. "Do you have any idea how wonderful your mother is? Up until a few weeks ago, because nobody knew when Gwen would wake up, it was sometimes months and months before anyone even talked to her. When she did wake up, often no one was even here before she would fall asleep again. But your mom started leaving pictures and notes for her so that when she woke up, she would know the world hadn't forgotten her.

"The thing that surprised all of us is that Gwen wrote back. She wrote me too. Thank you, Cath. Thank you." Pattie hugged her.

Now, hugs are funny things. Some are awkward or meaningless, like when someone you just met or don't really like gives you one. Other times they are just a quick reminder of constant affection like when your kids hug you good night. But the best hugs heal you, like when a mother hugs her young child who is afraid or sick, and suddenly everything is okay again. When Pattie hugged Cath, that is how it felt, and she knew that she had found a true friend.

"Can I write her?" Sandra asked.

"Sure." Pattie got some paper, and Sandra rustled through the crayon bucket to find a bright red crayon. Before long they were each busy writing their own messages.

By the time mother and daughter headed back to the car half an hour later, Sandra seemed pleased with herself. She reached over and gave her mom a light squeeze. "That was really neat, Mom. How come you never told me about her?"

Cath shrugged. "There are a lot of good things you don't know about me."

"Well, I know something about you that you don't," replied Sandra.

"What's that?" she asked lightly.

"Your mascara's smudged—I mean, raccoon-face level."

✳ hawaiian charades

By the time the groceries were unloaded and the house was pulled together, it was almost time to light the coals. Mike and Carson were jumping on the trampoline, Sandra and her mother were cutting up the salad and relish, and Kevin and Jordan were playing with fire. Although they had briquettes, Kevin discovered they were out of lighter fluid, and rather than making a trip to the store, he had decided to use gasoline. Cath had vowed not to even watch when suddenly Jordan came running in the back door. "Mom, you should have seen it—it was incredible!"

"What?" she asked, only half interested.

"When Dad poured the gasoline on the fire, the flame started climbing up the stream and would have blown up the whole gas can if he hadn't capped it off the way he did. It was brilliant." Jordan was filled with admiration.

Just then Kevin came in smelling like a garage and began soaping up his gas-soaked hands. "Don't worry; we have things completely under control." Cath peeked around the corner and could see the three-foot column of fire rising from the small barbecue but said nothing.

"The coals will take a little longer to get ready. We have to make sure that all the gasoline has burnt off, but it will be fine.

Trust me." Kevin dried off his hands and ran outside to chastise Mike and Carson for throwing pinecones in the fire. Cath silently wondered if every boy was born with the pyromaniac gene or if it only ran in her family.

Jerri and Bishop Miller arrived right at six, and everyone rushed to the back porch, where a large cooler was filled with ice and cans of soda. Sandra quit making her salad to join the fun, leaving neat piles of finely cut up vegetables spread across the counter and only half the tomato diced. Cath was left to finish it alone and was getting ready to dump everything in a bowl when the doorbell rang again, and there stood Pattie. She had brought a bottle of non-alcoholic champagne and had a nervous look in her eyes. As Cath gratefully took it from her, she said, "Welcome! The fun is on the back porch. I'm still finishing up in the kitchen, but I'll be out in a jiffy."

"Then I'll help you in the kitchen." She smiled and followed Cath around the corner. Cath let her finish the salad while she cleaned up. When she turned around, she couldn't believe her eyes. Pattie had swirled the vegetables into a pattern that looked almost like an Indian sand painting. "You are so talented. That's amazing," Cath couldn't help saying.

"Thanks," Pattie replied modestly. They finished laying out the last of the condiments and headed to the back porch. As the two women opened the back door, the boys were all on the grass with Jerri, sparring with large sticks. She was facing Jordan on one side and Carson on the other with Mike cheering her on, waiting for his turn. The loud thwack of wood against wood made Cath nervous for her sons, who seemed totally unaware that their attacker could have taken them at anytime. Cath guessed Jerri's plan was to let them wear themselves out before she went in for the kill.

Meanwhile, Kevin and the bishop were nursing his large column of fire, which seemed to still be going strong, and Sandra sat on the porch looking frustrated. Catching sight of Pattie, she leapt from her seat. "I'm so glad you came!"

Bishop Miller stood up and waited to be introduced. Sandra faced him. "This is Miss Pattie Wilson, and she designed the Lutheran Childcare Center but is now looking into our church. She is awesome! And this is Bishop Miller. He is the bishop. That's sort of like the pastor."

"Really," said Pattie. "So is your wife like the vice-bishop? I mean, do you lead together?"

Sandra was sitting down next to Pattie, happy to finally be included. "No, she doesn't even come anymore," Sandra said without thinking.

"Why is that?" Pattie asked Bishop Miller seriously.

"That's a good question." Jerri had come up to the porch to meet the new guest, and they hadn't noticed that she was right there. Cath felt terribly embarrassed, but Jerri just sat down looking nonplussed and took a quick swig of her soda. "I'm Jerri," she shook Pattie's hand amiably, "and you are . . ."

"Pattie, Pattie Wilson. I hope the question isn't too personal. I was curious. After all, it would have to be something pretty big to make the wife of the head of your church not go. I just want to know both sides." Pattie looked at Jerri with sincere interest, and Cath marveled at these two brave and honest women.

Jerri shook her head, laughing. "Something pretty big, now that is funny. I haven't really given it much thought in years, but the truth is it wasn't something big at all. It was something small and stupid, but isn't that the way it always is? We never trip over boulders; it's the small stones that get in our path that make us end up flat on our face."

"Do you still believe it's true?" Pattie asked.

"I know it is. There is no question in my mind and I'd never deny it. I just had the wind knocked out of me one too many times." Jerri shook her head, trying to lift the weight of dark memories from her mind, and looked to her husband, who sat quietly and put a supportive hand on her knee. "So, Pattie, what do you do?" she asked, changing the subject.

"Nothing at the moment," Pattie answered softly.

This conversation seemed to be dancing on everyone's sore spots, and as the hostess, Cath decided to intervene. "Actually, Pattie is a fabulous artist and was the founder and director of the Lutheran Childcare Center until a few weeks ago. She is very talented."

"Really? I've heard great things about that place." Jerri leaned back more comfortably. "My company was contracted to review their procedures but the service was cancelled. Do you know anything about that?"

Pattie's mouth dropped open. "I can't believe they cancelled; we've been on the waiting list for four months. There are some unique situations that need to be resolved with the duct work and the glass partition. If they let it continue to deteriorate, they'll have thousands of dollars of damage on their hands, and they may have to shut down."

"Wait, I thought you owned a cleaning business, Jerri," Cath interjected.

"You're the owner?" Pattie said in awe. Jerri nodded modestly, and Pattie explained to the other questioning faces, "UCR, the United Cleaning Reserve, defines cleaning processes for institutions like hospitals, childcare facilities, and schools. They are the very best at what they do."

Jerri laughed. "You sound like a television ad."

"Jerri's too modest," Bishop Miller added. "She travels all over the country and has received hundreds of awards for her work."

"I couldn't do it without Kirt here." Jerri smiled at her husband. "He stays available to help whenever I need him. Last week he took off the entire week to fill in for a sick employee."

"Well, Jim is great about letting me off, and Rick took double shifts to fill in. Those guys are the best out there; we all went to high school together. Man, I'm going to miss it when I retire next year, but I know that Jerri will keep me plenty busy."

"You got that right." Jerri nodded.

Cath thought of Alexia's words about the bishop's low-paying job and felt bad that she had even wondered about it.

"You know," Jerri continued, "I was working in the hospital in the next town over, and they are looking for a designer to revamp their children's cancer wing. I could put in a good word for you."

Pattie nodded. "That would be great."

The boys hopped up on the back porch, tired of their game, and circled Jerri. "Hey, I thought you were supposed to bring the games?" they said.

"I assumed we were going to wait until after we ate," Jerri answered, looking to Kevin.

"Oh, that could be a while," he replied, adding more coals to the white ash residue of his inferno. "Why don't we play first?"

Jerri stood up and all the boys sat down in a row, watching her. "I thought we would try playing Hawaiian charades."

The boys crinkled up their noses like something smelled bad. "What? That sounds like a sissy game."

"You will be given a four-letter word," she said, pulling some slips of paper from her pocket, "and you have to turn around and spell out the letters using only your butt. Like a hula dancer." She turned around and wiggled her hips, and the kids all burst into laughter. Pattie raised her eyebrows and Cath giggled nervously, not sure how this looked.

Carson went first, spelling *runs* with his hips and then running in place to spur the group on. Then Sandra did *good*, which they got right away. Next, Jerri asked Pattie to take one. She got up and carefully spelled the letters b-a-l-l, and then she jumped in the air and made a swishing motion with her hips. Everyone called out *ball*, but she shook her head and repeated the same thing, jumping higher and swishing harder. Jordan yelled, "Bouncy ball?" Pattie was shaking her head violently, and the group was all laughing so hard that tears were rolling down their faces. Finally, she couldn't keep it in any longer. "I was dotting the *I* and crossing the *T*. It was b-a-i-t!"

At almost midnight they said their good-byes. Jerri and Pattie had exchanged numbers, which Cath was really happy about. She couldn't remember a time when she had laughed more since they had moved here. Pattie was the last to go, and as Cath walked her to the door, she said softly, "Thank you so much for having me. This was exactly what I needed." And Cath had to agree.

✹ an unknown intruder

When Cath opened her eyes Sunday morning, she saw something she had never seen before. Jordan and Carson stood at the foot of the bed in their suits and pressed white shirts. Their hair was even styled, and it was ten minutes to seven. Cath sat up in total amazement.

"Mom, we want to go with Dad. He said he has to go early for something. I can watch them prepare the sacrament and stuff," Jordan said eagerly.

Still feeling groggy, she tilted her head to one side, remembering that Kevin had told her he was being called as executive secretary that morning. Cath knew it was a perfect calling for him because even though her husband was out of town a lot, he was always available by phone. It would keep him connected to the ward even when he was far away.

"Sure, but why are you going, Carson?"

"I'm bringing *Preach My Gospel*." He grinned.

Cath was impressed. "Have fun. We'll see you there."

"Yeah!" The two boys high-fived each other and rushed down the stairs to catch their father. Cath had the feeling that she had just been duped but couldn't put her finger on exactly how. After showering and throwing on her Sunday clothes, she went downstairs barefoot with still-wet hair and couldn't believe her eyes. Every inch of the kitchen was a disaster. They had been too tired to clean up the night before since dinner started after ten thirty, thanks to Kevin's inferno. Cath knew about the dishes in the sink, but now mounds of trash were strewn across the floor with little bits of shredded napkin everywhere. A two-liter bottle of root beer had tipped over, and the caramel-colored contents covered the counter and dripped on the floor, aging through the night into a thick syrup. The ketchup and mustard were also knocked over with the nozzles chewed, and a half-eaten ice cream cone sat on the island, oozing out in a big puddle of swirled white and brown. The back door was wide open, and it was obvious that either a raccoon, a neighbor's dog, or both had done a job on the kitchen the previous night.

Totally oblivious to her surroundings, Sandra sat eating her morning cereal. Suddenly Cath realized why her sons had been ready to go so early, and she walked over to the back door, slamming it shut. Marching back into the kitchen, she grabbed a large garbage bag. "Sandra, start throwing as much as you can from the floor and counters into this bag. I've got to get Mike in the bath and then I'll be back to help you. We've got to work fast or we will be late for church."

"But, Mom, it's not my job," whined her daughter.

Looking around at the mess, Cath lost it. "Do you eat here? Do we provide a roof over your head? How dare you! Get to work this instant. You should have been working the minute you saw the kitchen. Do you think I am your personal slave?"

Sandra grabbed the bag angrily and started shoving everything in it, including the mustard and ketchup bottles and a dishrag, out of rebellion. Cath marched out of the kitchen, fuming. She was frustrated with the boys, too, who could have told her about the kitchen an hour ago but were too focused on avoiding helping to spill the beans. Well, at least she knew who was doing lunch dishes. Turning the corner, Cath stood and stared at Mike's made bed in the boys' room. He never made his bed without encouragement. Calling Mike's name, she hustled to the bonus room. He wasn't there either, so she headed back to her room, thinking he had probably climbed into her bed while she was downstairs. He wasn't there. No, this didn't make any sense. Running downstairs she called louder and looked in the office, the living room, and out back.

The deck was almost as dirty as the kitchen, but she knew it could wait until the next day. Walking around the outside of the house, she called for Mike and then went into the basement, which was only used for storage. She checked around moving boxes and shelves, growing more and more worried.

Trying to keep her frantic emotions in check, Cath went up to the kitchen and asked Sandra when she had seen Mike last. Cath remembered Carson kissing her good night while the adults were still talking out back and had just assumed Mike had gone to bed at the same time. She'd been too tired by the time the guests had left to do her regular walk through to check on the children and had gone straight to bed. Sandra couldn't remember seeing him at all after Hawaiian charades. He might have been playing with them, but no single incident stuck out in her mind. At that, Cath began to get frantic, wondering if he had been abducted twelve to fifteen hours before. What sort of a mother wouldn't even know?

Soon Sandra and her mother were yelling his name at full voice while combing the entire house—under every bed, in every closet, in the attic, and anywhere they could think of on the remote chance he was hiding as a joke. Sandra even walked the property line to see if he was trapped in a tree or had fallen asleep outside. Every moment felt like an hour as they searched, and Sandra arrived at the back door sweaty and panting with a worried expression on her face. "Mom, he's not outside. Could he have drowned in the potty pond?" Cath took a deep breath and pulled out the phone book.

"Pleasant Valley Police Department Dispatch. How may I direct your call?" the operator answered.

"I'd like to report a missing child—Mike Reed, he's four." Her voice began to quiver, and she hoped she'd be able to hold it together. A car was dispatched, and Cath called her husband's cell phone ten minutes after sacrament meeting had started. He answered on the fourth ring with a whisper. The only words she could get out were "Mike is missing" before falling into a blubbering mess. Kevin promised he would be home as soon as he could, and the police car arrived as Cath was hanging up. She opened the front door, wiping her tear-streaked face with her free hand, to a small older man who she recognized as the officer that had brought Sandra home.

He introduced himself. "Officer Beckman, Mrs. Reed."

She led him through the kitchen and into the front room. As they passed by the mess, he raised his eyebrows. She just said, "We had visitors last night."

"Of the human variety?" he snapped back lightly.

"We had a party and the back door was left open," Sandra explained. Recognizing the officer, she sputtered, "Y-you brought me home . . ."

"Yes." The officer sat down and took out his notebook and pen. "Let's start with background information, please. Could I first get the names and ages of each of the children in your family?" He continued to ask basic background questions like how long they had been in the house, where they had moved from, and what Kevin's employment was. As Cath answered, she was becoming more and more frustrated, thinking that they were wasting valuable time not looking for Mike. Finally he turned to her and asked, "How long has your son been missing?"

"We don't know," she spat at him. "Last night we had a small party and he was playing with us, but no one remembers seeing him or not. We got to bed so late that the children had put themselves to sleep, and I didn't kiss them good night and count heads like I normally do. It could have been yesterday afternoon or late last night. We can't be sure. This is why I'm so upset. I don't know where he is or how long he has been gone. He's only four. Mike is such a sweet kid. He wouldn't ever wander away from the house without an older brother. I don't think he has spent a minute alone in his entire life."

The words flooded from her mouth faster and faster. Sandra stared at her mother in shock, amazed by how much Cath loved her son. Cath tried to slow down her mind by taking a deep breath and looking away from the officer, when there, standing in the doorway, was her baby. She jumped from her seat and scooped him up into her arms, hugging him with such force that he could barely breathe.

"Mike, Mike!" she cried, with huge sobs of relief. After a few moments she put him down and frustration started filling in the place where worry had been. "Where have you been? We've been looking everywhere for you!" she stated sternly.

Mike looked around with wide eyes and said softly, "Last night Carson and I were playing hide and seek, and I hid in the best place in the world and fell asleep. I just woke up." He began to tear up, and the police officer moved in. He squatted down and addressed the boy directly. "Young man, I am a police officer. See my badge?" He held it out and Mike touched the ornate medal. "Would you mind showing me this perfect hiding place so that I can write it down for my records?"

Mike stood up straight and saluted. "Yes, sir." He turned and marched out to the garage, which, Cath suddenly realized, was the only place they had overlooked in their search. On the large wooden shelves that held the camping gear, there was a distinct indentation among the sleeping bags. It actually looked like a very comfortable place to spend the night.

As they walked out of the garage, Kevin drove up at top speed, screeched the car to a halt, and leapt out the door. He jogged up to them quickly. "What happened? Where is he?"

Officer Beckman stepped forward. "It seems that there was no cause for alarm. Your son just found a really good hiding place and almost terrified your wife to death. It looks like my work here is done. Good luck to you." He shook her husband's hand and then turned to Cath. "If you hurry, you should still be able to catch the last of your church meetings. Have you had a chance to notice that organ yet?"

Suddenly, she remembered that first day at the Lutheran day care. "Yes, I even played it and it is as marvelous as you say," she smiled.

"Lucky lady," the officer said.

"What is all this about?" Kevin said, feeling left out of the conversation.

"You mean, your wife hasn't told you about your wonderful organ?" The officer laughed.

"Our organ? With old, deaf Sister Witherby playing it, who could tell whether it was good or not. She only hits half of the right notes—it's awful." Sandra laughed.

"Why doesn't Mrs. Reed here play?" the officer asked, looking at Cath. "I assume you're trained."

She blushed. "No, I'm really not very good and I only play the piano. I don't know what half the stops do."

"The transition is not difficult, easier still with a good teacher," the officer said, smiling.

Kevin looked at his wife. "That's not a bad idea. You'd have to start practicing again, but it might be good for you, Cath."

"Are you serious?" she asked, shaking her head. "Maybe at another time in my life, but not right now. As a matter of fact, we've got to run if we want to get to church at all today, but thank you so much, Officer Beckman. I'm sorry for the false alarm."

"Anytime." He smiled at Kevin, jumped in his little car, and drove away.

Cath walked into Relief Society just as Hillary Jacobs stood to give the lesson. She obviously had done very little in preparation and was simply reading the lesson from the book, but Cath perked up when she heard the title: "Coping with Stress in Our Everyday Lives." It was as though her entire morning was a perfect example of what not to do. The lesson quoted a talk from President Hinckley, which said, "There is too much of criticism and faultfinding with anger and raised voices." Cath remembered earlier that morning how she had lashed out at Sandra for not helping with the kitchen when it really hadn't been Sandra's fault or responsibility. In fact, they had hardly carried on a civil conversation since the move.

The lesson read on, "Let us work a little harder at the responsibility we have as parents. The home is the basic unit of society. The family is the basic organization of the Church. We are deeply concerned over the quality of the lives of our people as husbands and wives and as parents and children." Cath cringed as she thought how she didn't even know where her baby was all last night and how it must have looked to the police officer that had dealt with two of her children in less than two weeks.

Finally the lesson ended with the words, "May you kneel in prayer before the Almighty with thanksgiving unto him for his bounteous blessings. May you then stand on your feet and go forward as sons and daughters of God to bring to pass his eternal purposes, each in your own way." She blinked back a tear and realized that this was the missing piece. She knew the answer to her struggles was in prayer. When she first found Mike gone, why didn't she think to pray first, and then look for him? Perhaps then she would have remembered the garage.

Her mother used to tell her that without asking the Lord for what we need, we really don't have the right to be upset if we don't get it. Cath considered how every miracle Christ performed was asked for. The ten lepers cried to the Lord, "Have mercy on us." The friends of the man with palsy carried him to the roof and ripped it apart so that he could be healed. The woman with the issue of blood fought her way through a crowd just to touch his garment. Cath sat humbly thinking of all her struggles with the move and sadly had to admit that she hadn't been as consistent with her prayers as she normally was.

As the lesson ended and they bowed their heads in prayer, Cath said her own prayer in her heart. She prayed that she could draw closer to Sandra. There was still a distance between them that concerned her. She prayed that she would be able to mend the rift she had created with Hillary and how sorry she was for not being more in control. She prayed for Pattie, that she would be willing to search out the truth and move forward with her life. As the prayer closed, Cath felt a gentle peace fill her for the first time since the move.

The door had opened and closed a number of times during the prayer since Relief Society had gone a few minutes over. As she stood up, Cath looked to the back of the room. There by the door stood Pattie with a nervous expression on her face. It almost seemed like a miraculous answer to Cath's prayer. The moment Cath saw her, she brightened and ran over. "Pattie, how great to see you!"

"Darn, I thought Jerri said it started at one."

"No, the block of meetings starts at ten." Hillary was standing beside them with a large binder in her arms.

Cath smiled at Hillary and turned to her friend. "This is Hillary Jacobs, the secretary of the Relief Society. If you want to know anything, this is the woman to ask. Hillary, this is Pattie, a dear friend of mine."

Hillary shook Pattie's hand and opened her book. "Are you visiting or have you recently moved to the area?" Her tone was businesslike and Pattie seemed a little flustered. "Well, neither. I have lived here all my life and just decided to come and check it out."

"Oh, you're an investigator! Well, let's see. Have you met the missionaries yet?" Hillary led Pattie into the hall and introduced her to the elders with Cath following behind as a third wheel. Within ten minutes, Hillary had made sure the missionaries had set her up for a first discussion and had invited Pattie to Enrichment Night that Tuesday. As she turned to leave, Hillary turned to Cath. "By the way, Sister Witherby can't make it on Tuesday, so we would like you to do the music for us that night. I hear you play."

Cath was caught off guard and smiled. "Sure, I'd love to."

"Great, we're learning about Joseph Smith. The opening hymn will be 'Joseph Smith's First Prayer' and the closing will be 'Praise to the Man.' See you on Tuesday; don't forget." With that, Hillary marched away.

Cath thought about the bass line of "Praise to the Man" and swallowed nervously. "Wow, she seems like a very friendly person," Pattie said. Cath nodded silently.

As the family walked in the kitchen door from church, the phone was ringing. There was no smell of cooking roast to greet them, and the room was still covered with mess. Discouraged, Cath quickly picked up the receiver, hoping to beat the machine. "Hello, this is Cath Reed."

"It's Sonja from the senior center."

"Sonja, what is it? Is Gwen all right?" Cath answered, worried.

"She's fine. Actually, she woke up last night and I got to talk to her. I've been trying to catch you but haven't been able to get through." Her voice sounded weak.

"We've been at church. What did Gwen say when you talked to her?" Cath asked anxiously.

"It was funny. She wanted to hear every detail of our conversation. I told her about it and how I'd started praying and she asked what I was praying for. Well, I laughed at her and asked what she meant. She told me that there are really only three reasons to pray. Gwen said the first reason to pray is to just to thank him. The second reason is to ask what he wants us to do—like what's my next step—and the third is to ask for the will or the knowledge to do it. So I asked—I asked what my next step is."

Cath hesitated and then couldn't wait any longer. "And?"

"I think I need to find my sister. I'm ready for that. I'm just not sure how," Sonja answered.

"Is she a baptized member?" she asked.

"Yes." Sonja sounded unsure of where Cath was going with this.

"I think there is a way to search for her records through the Church. The bishop could probably help you with that. Now, she may have been like you and become lost, but if she is active or even has her records current, it could help."

"Sure, I'm willing to give it a try. Do you have the bishop's number?" Sonja asked hopefully.

Pointing to the ward list taped to her cupboard, Cath read the number aloud. Sonja thanked her and said good-bye.

✹ not close to perfect

Tuesday morning was becoming more and more stressful. The children missed the bus, and then Kevin forgot to leave his church key on the window sill for Cath to use. Cath had pulled out the ward directory and was dialing her fourth number when she caught sight of it on the kitchen counter.

This was going to be Mike's last day of preschool. The center was going entirely full-time and was doubling rates for half-day students to pressure them out. It was just as well, but Cath was grateful for this last day. She had planned on using the time to brush up on the piano at the church so she wouldn't embarrass herself in front of Pattie and the entire Relief Society that night at Enrichment. She would attempt the organ in private, but Cath knew there was little chance she would be brave enough to play it and would probably simply use the piano.

By the time she got back to her room to change, it was almost ten. Cath decided to skip the shower and threw on a pair of jeans so that she could get Mike to preschool on time and make good use of every minute practicing. She was just walking out the door when the phone rang. It was the high school. They needed to talk to her right away. With a lump in her throat, she jumped in the car, dropped Mike off, and headed to the school. As she rounded the corner to the principal's office, she saw Sandra sitting on a chair. Her daughter would not meet her eyes, and Cath proceeded to the receptionist curiously. She was ushered into Principal Hill's office. He seemed like a reasonable man; he had a short beard and looked more like a psychologist than an educator. Cath had no idea what the meeting was about and watched her daughter disappear as the door closed.

"Are you aware that we have a closed campus policy at Pleasant Valley High School?" he asked. Cath nodded and he continued, "Apparently your daughter is not. She was caught by the local police station at the Jacobs's house, filling their trees with toilet paper. A childish prank, but when she was found, she was wetting the paper down with a hose. I am not sure about the history driving this activity, but, given that I know Zee quite well, I can guess."

Cath was speechless and hurt. How could Sandra be going through so much and share none of it with her? She felt like she was losing her daughter and was helpless to stop it. Principal Hill looked at her understandingly. "It's not that bad, but we would like to keep her for the rest of the day. She will be released at the normal time."

"May I speak with her?" Cath asked impatiently.

"Certainly. I'll give you a few minutes alone." Principal Hill left and a moment later Sandra walked in the room. Cath was filled with anger, sorrow, frustration, and bewilderment. She stared at her daughter like she was a stranger and implored with her whole heart, "Sandra, what is going on? Just tell me. What were you thinking?"

"Mom, it wasn't me."

"What are you talking about? They said they caught you at Zee's house. Why would you do such a thing? It's not like you."

"You don't understand anything about me. You never listen to me. It wasn't me, Mom," Sandra said, then started crying. "I don't know why I even try to talk to you." She crossed her arms and plopped in the chair, staring furiously at her mother until the principal opened the door.

Cath shook her head and walked out, feeling old and weighted. As she made her way to the door, a familiar face walked by her. It was Mr. Ryder in a hair net. She turned and followed him with her eyes, not quite believing what she was seeing. He stared back at her with a look of total hatred, not unlike her daughter had moments before. She decided to drive over to the Jacobs's house to check out the damage. The amount of toilet paper used on the small front yard was truly amazing, and the hose had left it wadded in the trees. The front storm door was written on with lipstick and read, "Cheater. Liar. Jerk." Hillary had a rake out and was struggling ineffectively to pull the long strands from the branches above her. Once she touched them, the wet paper would break, visibly frustrating the strained woman. Contritely, Cath got out of the car, grabbing handfuls of paper as she approached. "I am so sorry about this."

When Hillary saw her, she was livid. "How dare you come on my property. Hasn't your family done enough damage for one day?"

"We will clean it up. I'll bring the boys over right after school," Cath promised, but Hillary shook her head. "Oh, no. I won't have any of your kids near my place. Since the first day you moved in, your family thought they were so much better than us. You butter yourself up to the bishop and bring investigators to church and think you are so wonderful, but you're not. Your investigator stood up the missionaries this morning. That's where I was when your daughter did this—pretty ironic, don't you think?"

Cath felt terrible. She climbed back in the car, defeated. The chances that she could repair this relationship were over, and Pattie had backed out. Nothing was working. Cath suddenly felt overwhelmed. She needed to talk to someone—to figure out what to do. She couldn't call Kevin; he was in meetings all day. The empty ache in her heart returned as she again grieved for her mother. She was alone. Thinking about it was agonizing, when Cath realized that there was not a single person in this entire community that she could call a true friend right now. Putting the car in gear, Cath drove aimlessly and found herself in front of the nursing home. She got out of the car, thinking at least Sonja would be there. When she walked up to the reception desk, Cath paused. A girl sat behind the desk who didn't look older than Sandra. "May I help you?" she asked cheerily, smacking her gum.

"Where's Sonja?" Cath stuttered.

"Oh, she quit yesterday. Can I help you?" Cath shook her head, ready to turn and head back home. As an afterthought she said, "I've come to see Gwen Keen." The girl buzzed her in and Cath slowly trudged down the hall. Everything she had hoped for had been a waste. Pattie was not going to accept the gospel. Hillary would make church worse than ever for her, and Sandra was almost totally lost. Even Sonja had left without saying good-bye. Cath toyed with the idea of driving back to Utah that night. She knew staying at her parents' house would be difficult on her father, but he'd be fine with it until they found a place of their own.

"Oh, Mom, I wish you were still here," she whispered to the stale air. She couldn't bear living there for one more minute. She would just leave, and maybe then she could win Sandra back and start over again. It would be devastating for Kevin's career, but didn't her feelings matter? Didn't anyone care about her?

Cath stood in the doorway, facing Gwen's closed door. She felt trapped in a cloud of cold gray emptiness. With nowhere else to turn, she paused and silently bowed her head before the closed door and prayed to Heavenly Father for help.

✸ finally awake

When Cath finished her prayer, she didn't feel any better—as a matter of fact, she felt worse. Praying in front of a closed door felt symbolic of her life at the moment, and she angrily pushed the barrier away from her. It slapped against the wall, making a loud thwack, which caused the woman sitting up in bed in front of her to startle in surprise and drop a few of the letters she was reading. Cath ran forward, collecting the letters to hand back to the woman. Cath's heart was pounding as she stood with her arm outstretched, letters in hand, staring in bewilderment. Gwen's eyes were light blue like the sky on a spring morning. There was such a kindness to her brow. Cath had so much to say to her, she didn't know where to begin when Gwen asked, "Yes? Do I know you?"

It was like the wind was just knocked out of her. Cath had forgotten that Gwen had never seen her before. She really didn't know her at all. She suddenly realized that this whole thing was all simply her own fantasy. What was she doing here, bothering this woman who didn't even know her? Why would Gwen want to be burdened with her problems? She turned, ready to go, when Gwen called out, "Wait, could you please come and visit with me for a moment?" Cath cringed and knew she couldn't refuse. Turning back, she sat timidly on the chair by Gwen's bed.

Smiling down at her visitor, Gwen stared at every facet of her face, trying to remember. Cath was determined to be contained but couldn't help it and began to cry. The tears streamed softly down her cheeks and she bowed her head. This was a bad decision, she thought, embarrassed by her behavior. How could she burden this frail woman with her problems? What was she thinking?

After a long time, Gwen said, "You're Cath, aren't you?"

Cath nodded silently and looked up. Gwen was smiling at her tenderly. "Do you know all the good you have done?"

Her question stung like salt in an open wound, as she looked back on all that had happened since the move. Cath wanted to be agreeable. She would simply lie to this woman who she had never really met before, leave, and go back to Utah—start over. But then she looked up into Gwen's honest blue eyes, and she knew she had to tell the truth. Cath shook her head and whispered, "No."

Gwen reached out her hands. "Come here," she said. Cath obediently stood and Gwen reached her arms around her and hugged Cath close to her heart. If her own mother had been there, she would have done the same thing, and after a while Cath could feel a calmness finally rest upon her. "It will be all right," Gwen crooned softly.

Cath pulled back, shaking her head. "But it's all gotten so crazy." The words poured out of her mouth. "Kevin is always traveling and I miss him so much. I talked to Pattie about church before I even got to know her, and now I don't think she will ever look at it again. I have half the Relief Society hating me because of Hillary Jacobs and the other half now hating Hillary Jacobs because of me. I've done so much good with Sonja that she didn't even contact me before she left town, and I'm such a terrible mother that my own daughter won't even talk to me. I'm so afraid for her."

Gwen gently touched her cheek. "Cath, you are so wonderful. Do you know what I hear?"

"The blubbering of a crazy lady?" Cath asked.

"No," Gwen smiled, "I hear the sound of love. Every concern out of your mouth was for another. You have a huge heart and actually remind me a lot of myself."

"How?" Cath sniffled.

"When I was teaching, how I loved my kids. They became a part of me, but I only had control over those few hours that they were in my classroom. Every year there would be one or two of my students who I could tell came from miserable circumstances. All night I would worry about them, to see them the next morning come with a new bruise or, worse, day by day watch them disappear inside themselves from neglect. After my fifth year of teaching I was almost ready to quit, because I couldn't handle the deep sorrow I felt for these defenseless children that I loved. That was the year that the prophet told us to plant a garden, remember? You were probably just a child then. Well, when he said those words, it was like he said them just for me. It became my answer. Whenever I worried, I would work in the garden, and with my hands busy, my mind was somehow lifted of its burden. It recharged me, and I could continue to love and serve. I taught for another twenty years."

"Wow," Cath said admiringly, "you are incredible."

"Cath, look at yourself. You are running on empty right now. You need something that is going to allow you to have the strength to do all you're supposed to in this life. I know the Lord has a great plan for you, but you can't do it in your current state. You need to be strong for your children, for your friends, and for the Lord. Now tell me about the organ. When was the last time you played it?"

"The organ?" Cath asked surprised. That seemed like a pretty far leap. Ironically, she was supposed to be practicing it right then so that she could play it that night. "I don't understand what that has to do with it."

"Don't you remember your one fun thing? The organ could be

your garden. When you get really worried or upset, if you just sat down and filled the room with music, do you think it might help?" Gwen grinned.

"But I'm terrible. I can never even make it through a hymn on the piano without mistakes. Add the foot pedals and you can barely tell which song I'm playing," Cath confessed.

"The first year I started my garden, it was a disaster. The only things that grew were radishes and Swiss chard. Everything else either withered as a seedling or was eaten by rabbits and raccoons. But every year I learned a little more, built up my fence, found out what grows well in this area, and by my third year, I had something to be proud of. It may take you years, but not only will it feed you, it will bless others."

Cath thought about her words and nodded. "But what about Sandra and Pattie?"

"You need to know as long as we do our part, Heavenly Father will work out the details in his own due time." Gwen smiled. "You know, God really does move in mysterious ways. I don't know how much Pattie has told you about her past, but I don't think she would mind me telling you this. When I first had her in my class, she was one of those children I worried so much about. One rainy day I was out in my garden—I felt compelled to be there despite the weather. I had gone into the garage to grab a hoe when I saw her walking on the sidewalk in front of my house, soaked to the skin. I invited her in and we had hot chocolate and talked until late into the afternoon. It began a sweet relationship that has blessed both of our lives, all because I listened."

Gwen leaned back and closed her eyes. "Cath, just listen to the Spirit. It will guide you to do the things you should and leave the rest in the Lord's hands."

Cath reached up and touched her silver dove necklace and remembered that Kevin had told her the same thing. Was all her concern really just a lack of faith?

Gwen touched Cath's hand. "I wish we had more time to talk, but I'm so tired. Just know that I love you for making me feel alive again. Maybe this was the reason God wanted me to hang around. You are a great woman. Always remember that and take this—it may help."

Cath took the folded paper and held Gwen's hand gently. "Thank you so much," she whispered, but she wasn't sure if Gwen heard. Gwen's breathing had grown slow and steady. She had fallen asleep again. Looking down at the letter Gwen had given her, Cath bent back the top flap, exposing little crayon hearts. It was from Sandra.

✿ planting a garden and getting rid of the weeds

That night when Cath pulled into the church parking lot an hour before the meeting began, three cars were already there. Sandra sat beside her in the car, feeling awkward about being forced to attend, but Cath wasn't letting her out of her sight until they had time to talk—really talk. "I've been so lonely that I made some bad choices," the letter had read. "I feel like I've hurt the relationship between my mother and me, which makes me sad because I really need her right now. I just don't know how to fix it." Cath could see in Sandra so much of herself. She knew what it felt like to need her mother and not have her.

When Sandra had gotten home that afternoon on the bus, Cath didn't say a word—she had just held her daughter in her arms. She told her how much she loved her and was sorry she had been so distracted. Sandra, who was expecting to be disciplined, was shocked. Cath explained that she needed time to practice the organ before Enrichment Night, so she ordered a pizza for the boys and headed out as soon as possible with Sandra in tow.

They hurried through the church doors but were stopped by a woman they had never met before. The older woman's smile lit up the room and Cath immediately loved her.

"Hi, I'm Brenda Ramsey, the Relief Society president. I don't think we've met."

Cath remembered hearing that the president had been out of town helping her daughter with her first baby, but Cath had no idea when she would be back. "I'm Cath, and this is my beautiful daughter, Sandra," Cath said with an arm around her girl.

"We are so grateful you are in our ward. I've heard about all the wonderful things you've done. You have already touched so many lives for good—I really feel you were prayed here." Brenda's eyes were filled with sincerity, and Cath was taken aback, blushing at the kind words.

"That's my mom." Sandra smiled proudly.

Sister Ramsey encouraged Sandra to head into the cultural hall and help her with the rest of the decorations while Cath ducked into the chapel to practice.

By the time the meeting began, Cath felt confident with a few hymns and was playing a soft prelude on the organ. She'd concluded that "Praise to the Man" would definitely be a piano experience. The bishop and the Relief Society presidency were sitting on the stand, and Cath looked up briefly to see if Sister Ramsey was standing yet when Hillary walked by her, giving her the evil eye. Cath simply smiled and vowed before the night ended that she would try her husband's strategy and compliment her. They may never be close friends, but she could respect Hillary and just be polite.

The opening song was simple and Cath enjoyed using the foot pedals, only changing them every two or three measures. About fifteen women had come, and Pattie was not among them—that was an empty hope. After the opening prayer, Cath went back to the pews and sat next to Sandra. She whispered to her mother, "I can't believe how good you did."

Cath smiled. "It's the instrument; it is awesome to play. You've got to try it." Sandra gleamed at her mother and snuggled in under her arm as the bishop began speaking about Joseph Smith.

When it was time to head into the cultural hall for the activity, Cath and Sandra picked an empty table. Soon it filled with three other women. As they etched glass, Cath learned that almost everyone at her table had moved in about the same time she had. Sister Thomas had just moved from Arizona with her husband and seven children, and Emma Hansen was newly married but was not working, hoping to start a family. They had each had a difficult time connecting with anyone in the ward, and before the closing they had exchanged numbers to begin a walking group—really walking.

When Cath stepped up to the stand at the end of the evening, she suddenly felt a boost of confidence. Sitting at the organ, she opened the hymnal and pulled out all the stops as wide as they would go to blast the sound through the rafters. Cath kicked off her shoes and used every ounce of concentration to have her feet slap up and down the long boards while her fingers hit mostly the right keys. She had to drop a few notes and reached too far with her foot during one of the verses, making an obvious doinker, but even though it wasn't perfect, it was happy, bright, and full of love. As she held the last note and lifted her fingers from the keys, she closed her eyes and felt that her sacrifice was acceptable to the Lord. Cath suddenly realized that her performance was a pretty good reflection of her life. As she closed the lid of the organ, she felt that even though it wasn't perfect, she knew her mother was proud of her—and because of Christ's great gift, they would be together again.

After pulling into the driveway, Cath put her hand on the car door handle to get out when Sandra asked her mother to wait. "Mom, can you just listen now?"

Cath turned to her daughter and beamed. "I can do that." She sat next to Sandra and gave her 100 percent of her attention.

"Mom, it wasn't what you thought. Zee liked me, but we never really did anything. We never even kissed. I mean, he tried, but I told him no."

"Good for you." Cath vowed she would say as little as possible and stay positive.

"That day Zee was supposed to meet me when I got off the bus, and he wasn't there so I went looking for him. He was behind the school kissing another girl. I said I thought he was going out with me, and Jamie was as mad as I was. We both have second period together and it was her idea. I mean, I went along with it, and I'm sorry. We skipped third period, stole the toilet paper from the janitor's closet, and went to Zee's house with three of her friends. It felt so good to get him back, and it didn't seem like a really bad thing to do, but then Jamie got the hose out, and I thought that was just mean—and not even just mean to Zee but to his whole family, who would have to clean it up. I grabbed the hose from her just as Zee's mom drove up. The other girls ditched me and Sister Jacobs called the cops. I know I'm not perfect, but don't you see?"

"Sandra," Cath was relieved—it wasn't nearly as bad as she had imagined, "I'm so sorry all this happened to you."

"I'm not. I've learned so much, like who you hang out with has a big effect on who you become. I promise I'm not going to make that mistake again. Well," Sandra smiled, "maybe when I'm sixteen, but don't worry, it's not happening before then. Mom, there's one more thing."

"What?" Cath couldn't imagine anything that could make her happier, but Sandra found something. "Is there a time we can go to the mall? I've got some things I've got to return."

❋ loose ends and happy endings

For the next three weeks, life was pretty much back to normal. Cath hadn't heard from Jerri or Pattie, but she had gone walking every day with her new circle of friends and was given a new visiting teaching route with a real companion, although she still visited Gwen weekly. Unfortunately, Gwen had not woken up since that awful and wonderful Tuesday.

It was Friday afternoon, and the boys burst through the front door, threw down their backpacks at the base of the stairs, and ran up to the bonus room to start playing PS2 games. Sandra sat at the kitchen counter and laid three Oreos on a saucer and then poured herself a cup of milk. She picked up a cookie and held it in the milk until it got soft. Cath was busy at the sink finishing up the last of the breakfast dishes that she had avoided all day, choosing instead to spend her time finishing a Mary Higgins Clark novel that she had bought ages ago but never made time to enjoy. While putting away the last of the still-damp dishes, Cath heard Sandra softly say, "I like it here."

Cath nodded. "Me too."

"I mean, it took a while to get used to, you know?"

Cath laughed, "Boy, do I know, but you're right. It really feels like home." The phone rang and Sandra jumped up happily and grabbed the receiver. Suddenly her face fell. "Mom, it's for you. It's from the nursing home."

Cath listened in silence and then thanked the woman and hung up. Sandra asked what the matter was. Cath said, "Gwen's gone," and walked into the other room.

A few minutes later Kevin came home. Cath was sitting in the dark. She could hear Sandra telling her dad what had happened. He walked into the room solemnly and put his arm around his wife. "I'm so sorry, Cath. I know you were friends."

Cath nodded, thinking that "friends" did not describe their relationship. Gwen was a gift to her life and would be one of her greatest heroes, right next to her mom. She wondered if the two were talking together right now.

Kevin looked at her, concerned. "You know, Cath, I've noticed how hard this move has been on you, Sandra, and Carson—and now to have to deal with this. All I'm saying is that if it is too much, we can move back. I can find another job—the career is temporary, but our family is forever."

Cath looked at her dear husband and laughed softly. "If you had said that to me a few weeks ago, I might have taken you up on it, but, Kevin, this is where the Lord wants us to be and as long as we pull together, it will just make us all stronger," she said and hugged him. The doorbell rang and Carson and Jordan came dashing down the stairs, screaming, "Pizza! Pizza!" Cath smiled at Kevin. "And so it goes."

Three days later, Cath was putting on her lipstick. She called down the hall, "Hurry up, Sandra. Dad is already in the car, and we don't want to be late."

"Mom, can I wear your shoes? They'll match better," she asked, running into the bedroom and rummaging through the closet.

"You fit them?" Cath couldn't believe how much Sandra had grown. Putting her arm around her daughter, they dashed through the hall and out the front door to the waiting Buick and climbed into the backseat together, letting Kevin chauffeur them.

Sandra leaned her head against her mother's shoulder. "Mom, I'm having a hard time feeling sad. Aren't you always supposed to cry when someone dies?"

Cath thought about it. "I don't know. When someone has lived a very good life and their body is worn out, there is a whole different feeling, isn't there? I'm just feeling so grateful that we had the opportunity to share the few strands of time we were given together. I'll always remember her."

Sandra nodded as they turned into the half-filled church parking lot. Jerri and Bishop Miller stood at the front door welcoming everyone. Sandra hugged Jerri and asked why she hadn't come over to play for so long.

"Actually," she smiled, "I've been out of town, but I'm just about finished with my current project. What if we make a date for next weekend?"

Sandra wiggled her hips back and forth, looking to her dad excitedly. "I've been practicing Hawaiian charades."

Kevin chuckled and shrugged. "Sure, that would be great." And the deal was done. The one thing Cath knew for sure was that she was not serving hot fudge sundaes. They were about to go into the chapel when someone caught Cath's arm. She turned to see Pattie. "Can I speak to you for a second?"

Her stomach flopped over, but Cath nodded. Pattie led her to a corner while Kevin took Sandra and went ahead to find a seat. Cath looked into Pattie's eyes, trying to figure out what she was going to say. She seemed on the verge of tears, and Cath worried that she had caused her pain.

"I need to apologize for not contacting you while I've been away," she began.

"That's fine," Cath said a little too loudly, not completely covering her hurt.

"Things were so confusing when I left, and then I poured myself into the work, which has been more wonderful than I ever dreamed. Did Jerri tell you I've been working with her on that children's ward? I already have two more hospitals that want me to do remodels. It is exactly what I wanted to do with my life. But what I realized in the middle of it all was that it still wasn't enough. Something else was missing."

Cath shook her head, unsure where she was going with this.

"Two weeks ago I called the missionaries. Jerri and I sat through the first few discussions with them every night for the last two weeks. Jerri is a powerhouse; she has the most amazing testimony, and last week I went to the local ward. The people were just incredible. But it's not about the people—is it? It's about the Spirit and knowing it's true. That's what you tried to tell me, but I wasn't ready to listen. I get it now. Cath, I just need to thank you for everything. You are a true friend." Pattie hugged her, and Cath was glad she had worn waterproof mascara.

Cath caught sight of her watch and hurried to take her place on the stand. She was especially nervous and couldn't believe that she had actually volunteered to play, but she felt it was the best gift she could give to Gwen. Cath had found information about basic organ instructions on the Internet and had been working on practicing piano at home. She'd even gotten permission to play the organ on Wednesdays and Sundays. She smiled as she confidently adjusted the stops and began playing Pachelbel's "Canon in D." The simple melody sang through the room, clear and undefiled. It repeated with another opposing theme of notes below it. A third time it was joined by a more complex strain above, repeating again until the entire room was filled with sound and motion. But then, at the point where it was almost more than one could bear, each opposing melody began to resolve one at a time until once again the simple clear melody sang out more beautiful than it had at first.

Cath took a deep breath and began playing the hymn that had brought her so much solace—the first song she ever played on this organ. She followed the words with her eyes and was surprised because she had never read the last verse before:

Be still my soul: When change and tears are past,
All safe and blessed we shall meet at last.

Cath knew she would miss Gwen so much. She had been Cath's rock during this crazy time, and she felt Gwen was absolutely right when she had said that maybe the Lord had lengthened her life because he knew Cath needed her. Cath was filled with comfort and knew she would see her again.

The service was beautiful, and when it was done Pattie invited Cath and her family to her house for the wake. As they pulled up, Sandra was almost bouncing in her seat, pointing at the little luminaries lining the walkway leading to the back of the house, which looked like a giant bouquet peeking out over the little fence that surrounded the yard. The blossom-laden bushes and trees shouted with bright colors even in the late fall. As soon as they approached, Pattie threw her arms around the excited Sandra, and the two trotted off to talk about trees, flowers, childhood, and Gwen. Cath pulled closer to Kevin, and they were met by Jerri and Bishop Miller, who stood next to a familiar face. Jerri stepped up to make the introduction. "Oh, Cath, I don't know if you've met Pattie's fiancé?"

"Actually, we've met a number of times." Cath shook his hand awkwardly.

Jerri ignored Cath and turned to him seriously. "So are you and Pattie going to get married sometime soon or what? You aren't getting any younger."

Officer Beckman turned a little red and tried to change the subject. "Your organ playing was beautiful. I'm very impressed," he said, bowing to Cath.

"No, it was not that complex a number, and I am still so clumsy with my foot pedals," she said, embarrassed by his expertise.

"Mrs. Reed, each organist has their own voice. Mine may be technically superior, but in you there is a sensitivity and beauty that shines through your music. That is what you need to enjoy and allow to grow."

Suddenly Sandra appeared and threw her arms around her mother. "Mom, this place is awesome! Pattie says we can come over any time. It's just amazing to me that Gwen planted all of this."

"She was an amazing woman," echoed Pattie, "who taught me so much."

"What surprises me," interjected Ralph Beckman, "is that you never knew she was a Mormon. What do you think she would say now if she knew we were taking the discussions together?"

"Together?" asked Kevin.

Ralph nodded. "I am ashamed to say that I wouldn't even consider investigating your doctrines, and I even discouraged Pattie here. But when a friend of mine came to me spouting shameful things about your Church and a particular person here in our company . . ."

"That friend wouldn't happen to be an ex-teacher," Cath said under her breath.

The inspector looked down. "Ken Ryder is a good man, but he just takes things too far sometimes. I might have been as blinded as he is, but the more I got to know of your family, the more the dichotomy became unmistakable and so I felt obligated to look into it further. Thus far I have found nothing but truth." He raised his head thoughtfully. "You know, it's odd that all these years I mourned the loss of my organ, and the answer was that I simply should have followed it."

The group settled into comfortable small talk, and Bishop

Miller pulled Cath aside. "I have a message for you from Sonja Townsend, Gwen's nurse. She wanted to be here but couldn't make it; apparently she is starting school in Logan and is living with her sister there. She wanted to thank you, Cath—you and Gwen."

Cath was delighted by the news. The bishop asked her if she was ready for a calling. "We would like you to serve as ward organist. Sister Reed, I delayed calling you because I was thinking of putting you in another position, but I know this is where the Lord wants you. If you need help, I'm not sure what to tell you. We don't have a lot of resources in the music department."

She smiled. "That's all right. I actually think I've got someone in mind." She wondered if Ralph Beckman would give Sandra and her lessons.

Finally the bishop pulled something from his pocket. "Apparently, Gwen did wake for a few minutes before she passed away and wrote only one last letter. It was for you."

Cath gasped and took the treasured envelope from his hand. She walked silently back to a little grove, surrounded by blooming azaleas and honeysuckle bushes, and sat on a cast iron bench. The sweet gentle fragrance hugged her, and Cath imagined Gwen in this very garden and thought of all the effort and caring that she had put into every square inch. She carefully tore open the seal and unfolded the plain paper. The handwriting was unsteady. Cath read:

Dear Cath,

I didn't feel like we finished our conversation the other day. You said you were worried about Pattie, but I'm not. Pattie told me how you left the Ensign with her. She said that she felt the Spirit for the first time in her life. When we spoke together, I was able to do something I never have with her—bear my testimony. I always wanted to, but the time was not right. As a teenager, the church she was going to was the only constant in her life and then when she moved in she had just started the day care and it was her life. We may not have talked about the Church, but we often talked about the gospel.

It is funny what we think about out of the blue. When I woke up today I remembered a saucer of bulbs that I had forced to bloom. They were hyacinths in various colors, and I loved the way they filled the whole house with their exotic aroma. But forced bulbs only bloom once—they say. When they were done, I put them in a corner of my garage and forgot about them for years. One day I was finally cleaning out the corners and put the saucer out by the dumpster. That night it rained, and a few days later when it was time to bring the trash to the corner, I noticed they were sprouting. I brought them in, watered them a little more, and they blossomed again even more beautifully.

Thank you for being my rain. Thank you for letting me blossom one last time.

Gwen

christine edwards thackeray

After receiving her bachelor's degree in English from Brigham Young University, Christine married Greg Thackeray and had seven beautiful children—five boys and two girls.

Christine has had a diverse career. She has developed a phonics program used in private schools, authored several brochures and articles, worked as a technical writer, and completed many studies as a professional marketing analyst.

During that time, she always maintained a love of writing. *The Crayon Messages* is Christine's first novel. She has also assisted her sister Dr. Marianna Richardson with editing and research on her new book, *Alfred Edersheim: Jewish Scholar for the Mormon Prophets* in the *Spiritual Context—LDS Perspectives* series. Christine will be co-authoring future books in this series.